The Estate

THE ESTATE

The Wrightsville Series
by Annalee Thomasson

In The Moonlight
Coming Home
The Estate

The Estate
Copyright © 2020 Annalee Thomasson
KDP ISBN 9798683894955
Cover design by Annalee Thomasson, Wilmington, NC
Back cover author photo by Jana Tyler, Magnolia Photography,
Greenville, NC

THE ESTATE

DEDICATION

For my sweet kids.
I hope you grow to know that home is what you make it.
Home is who you love.
And there is *always* room for more.
I love y'all.

THE ESTATE

THE ESTATE

ACKNOWLEDGMENTS

Self publishing is no easy task, and neither is the writing. There have been many helping hands on the path to getting my books out there, and I want to extend an extra thanks to those of you who have encouraged me along the way.
I am incredibly thankful for each of you who has helped to spread my joy about these books.
Getting to spend time on something you enjoy is such a treat.
It's even better when you have people cheering you on.
Thank you, so much.

THE ESTATE

ONE

Ruby

Standing on the threshold of the front door to my childhood home, the memories came flooding back, and the only thing I could do was stop and soak it all in. It wasn't all that long ago that my parents had moved out of this house and into the new home that they built on the property next to my Uncle Eddy's. But a few months of vacancy, paired with the rotation of homeowners around here, made standing on this threshold feel like cracking open the lid to a time capsule.

If I looked closely enough, I could see Port dribbling a basketball on the kitchen floor, while mom fixed pancakes on a Saturday morning. I could hear my dad barging through the back door with a cooler full of the morning's catch, and Uncle Eddy just behind him claiming ownership of the biggest fish. If the rest of the kids were awake already, they were no doubt running around here somewhere on the row. Although, Penny was usually in close proximity to Port.

Cottage Row started out as a cafe with an upstairs apartment. But one by one, the homes popped up and the families grew. Before we knew it, two generations had come and gone, and now I was here to get it all back.

The cafe was still going strong thanks to my mom. She took it over when my Aunt Nori passed away, making sure we kept things in the family. It's where I spent most of my one-on-one time with my mom, since it was one of my many part time streams of income. When I wasn't behind the counter, I was also selling large canvas photo prints that we displayed on the walls.

Ryan and Lucas had spent a good majority of the past few years traveling, and their photography quickly proved to be a great source of funds to help them reach and enjoy the many locations on their bucket list.

Their photography hobby had turned into a lucrative enough business that one trip turned into two and then three, and four years later they were still sending me photos to print and sell in the cafe. They came home now and then, but otherwise had adopted that sort of gypsy soul we all had stuffed down deep inside somewhere. Some of us were just more attached to the idea of home than the others.

The twins weren't technically my brothers; they were Eddy's oldest. But from the outside looking in, no one really knew which kids belonged to which parent, and that's the way we liked it. The six of us were "frouslings". The nickname had come along at some point in reference to us being raised as friend-cousin-siblings. Although, I guess Penny and Port getting married made that a bit more official.

THE ESTATE

We used to refer to our combined family unit as *the herd*; and I was the youngest. I'd learned to walk on these floors, chasing the rest of them. I was the one who put the hole in the wall next to the refrigerator when I got my hands on Ryan's new spearfishing equipment one Christmas morning. Uncle Eddy patched it up, but it left a mark. Port had gotten locked out of this front door more times than I could count, and climbed through the living room window at all hours of the night, regardless of curfew.

I always kept quiet when I saw him sneak into the house after a late night out with Penny, usually spent down at the marina. I'd found them kissing once and kept my mouth shut about that too, even when mom pried for gossip. I didn't tell her about their wrestling either, especially when I grew up a little and realized they weren't really wrestling at all. Being eight years younger kept me naive to a lot.

Things on the estate were starting to pick up again now that Port held the reigns. My parents and Uncle Eddy decided they'd build their smaller, one level homes to retire in so that they could slow down, but stay close and be available to help as needed. I had been staying in one of the guest houses since graduation, but with Port's new ranch hand moving in, I was politely kicked out of the guest house and sent back here to Cottage Row. I didn't mind it though. In fact, it kind of made things seem full circle. This is the only place that ever really made sense to me.

Roger began handing the estate over to Port a while back and legally gave him the land and the business after graduation.

Roger said he wanted to keep it *in the family*, and no one argued. The definition of family around here was a loose term anyway, given the way we grew up. Penny loved the idea of moving home, so the two of them decided that this was a perfect solution to raise the boys here on the island like they wanted.

First, they moved into the guest house while Roger and Dana started to teach them the day to day operations of the property. Then when my parents built their new place, Port and Penny moved back in here to our childhood home on Cottage Row. This street served as the inland border of the estate. The chaos felt like musical houses around here, but now it was finally my turn.

Everything had been flowing pretty smoothly for a while now. When I graduated from Chapel Hill, the guest house was ready and waiting for me. It was supposed to be temporary, until I figured out a plan for my life. But, one by one I turned hobbies into jobs and before I knew it, juggling it all turned out to be the best plan all along.

So I decided to make it permanent. The estate stayed in the family, and I wanted the family to stay on the estate. As much as we could, at least. I had big plans for this house and was ready to work with Uncle Eddy to take the old run down cottage I grew up in and restore the charm and the shine I remembered. I didn't ever plan on leaving town, so I wanted to take the time to make it perfect for the long haul. Port even offered to fund the renovations with money from the estate, in hopes that one day he could rent out the houses on Cottage Row as vacation rentals. He really did have a lot of big ideas for this place.

THE ESTATE

A few afternoons a week, after a morning at the cafe with mom, I taught surf lessons. And if those part time jobs weren't enough, Port essentially gave me control of the stables; so I was working on getting a routine down, making sure I had a good handle on my assigned portion of the estate. If everything worked out and I was able to save enough money, I wanted to build my own place in the empty land by the gardens. But, that was a big dream, and it would take years to get there.

For now, I was home with a business degree. It seemed like a safe choice, even though I never did have any big plans to use it. I think my parents were a little irritated that I spent so much time on that degree to come back here and not put it to good use. But, thanks to my mom, the tourists, and Port, I had arranged a sort of combination career, made up of all my favorite things. If I had it my way, we'd be bringing a few more horses onto the property one day soon. For now though, I needed to show Port that I could handle what we already had before he'd let me add more to the plate.

Port had the business side of things under control, and knew the marina like the back of his hand. We learned how to handle the docks at a young age, running around as toddlers helping our dads keep the place clean. If we got into enough trouble, our punishment usually involved scrubbing a boat deck.

Penny was already plenty familiar with the gardens, and was able to learn more than the general maintenance over time. She was just getting to a point where she had the house and the boys into a working routine—"surviving, not thriving," she'd say—so other than the gardens, she didn't have room to take on

13

anything else.

That left the stables up to me, and admittedly, I'd set my sights a little high. If we could get a few rescues in here, and open up the stables to the public, I figured we could really turn a profit. Penny and I were also talking about creating an annual garden festival on the property. Maybe one day I'd put that degree to use after all.

The car horn sounding from the street startled me from my daydream. Uncle Eddy parked in front of the house; *my house*. He helped build this place a long time ago, back when there was only the cafe and his own house. The years had really changed things around here, and he had the gray hairs to prove it.

"Uncle Eddy! You made it." I ran to the sidewalk to meet him.

"Of course I did, kiddo. Wouldn't miss my favorite niece moving home. I hear you have big renovation plans." He pulled me under his shoulder, kissed my head, and then took us inside.

"I have a lot of ideas in mind, but I want to keep the charm of the place. I still want it to feel like home. I figure we owe it to your parents and Jane to try to honor the dreams they had for the Row, like you and mom and dad do now." I said, looking up all around the house.

"Lucky for you, this old man needs something to keep busy with. Your brother is finally getting enough hands on this place that your parents and I are starting to feel like we're actually a little bit retired."

"You're not that old, Uncle Eddy." I laughed.

"I'm not. Port seems ready for some hard work these

days, and I'm ready to give it to him. Besides, I could use a bit more time to fish and bother the guys down at headquarters with your dad. I'll be needing time to work on the house here with you anyway. You know you're my favorite." He winked and pulled a notebook out of his pocket and a pen from behind his ear. "Now, I was going to start making a list today. I'm pretty sure we'll at least need to fix a few leaky pipes, but that's easy. I know you've already moved in, but once you get settled, we can really dig in and tackle this place room by room."

"Well, I'm about as settled as I'll get. Port basically kicked me out of the guest house. He hired some new guy to basically move in and be his right hand man, so I got the boot and I got it fast." I'd intended to live in the guest house while I fixed this place up, but with Port's new staff moving in it looked like I was going to be living through a remodel instead.

I caught a glimpse at the time. "Shoot. Uncle Eddy, I have to go. I had a few more of the boys' pictures printed for the cafe, and I've got to pick them up. Mom and I were hoping to hang them up this morning. Oh, and hey, can you take the bucket on the porch over to the horses? I forgot their snack."

"Better get a routine down in those stables." He walked out onto the porch and picked up the bucket. "Port's never gonna let you bring more home if you can't keep up with what you've got." Our horses were so old that I was impressed when I found them up and walking around each day. As slow as they were, I loved spending time with them. They were sweet souls, and in their old age I was convinced that all they really needed were a few new friends.

He waved from the kitchen and got back to his list.

I got to the print shop right as Mrs. Keagy was unlocking the door for the day. I always ran my errands early in the morning, which seems normal when you operate on coffee shop hours. She handed my envelope full of prints through the open door.

"Right on time, Ruby." She had a smile only a grandmother could give, and I loved it.

"Thanks, Mrs. Keagy." I gave her a quick hug, and turned back toward the car. "I'll email you later this week! The boys are in the Cayman Islands!"

"Oh, I've always dreamed of such beautiful places." She leaned against the door frame with starry eyes. "I guess I can settle for some photos."

"You'll get there one day. And we can add your pictures to the wall." I winked and climbed back into my jeep.

As much as I loved everything I had going on, I refused to become one of those people who worked their life away for the money. Sure, I wanted to make enough to be comfortable. I wanted to save as much as I could, so that I could build my dream home. But what I really wanted was to live right here on the estate with my family, and do things like travel, see new places, and experience new things. I didn't want to get to Mrs. Keagy's age and have anything left undone. For the most part, I just wanted to roam the stables, the gardens, the cafe, and the waters around it all. It was the way I was raised, and the way I intended to spend the rest of my days.

My mom went through most days the same way, in addition to making sure my dad and Eddy didn't cause too much trouble. Aunt Nori was the same way, when she was alive. This is what our parents wanted for us. Life was just right, here. I guess to outsiders it might have seemed a bit lonely at times, but we had our family and most everyone on the island were close friends of ours.

Myself? I was on my own, though I got used to that in college. I was never the girl who dated, or partied, or had too much fun. I was there to get my degree and go.

It was good to be back. I always knew I would call the estate home again one day, and now it was. This was just the beginning for me, and everything was falling into place.

TWO

Hobie

Getting out of town isn't all that difficult when it's just you. Aside from the fact that I barely had anything to pack, I didn't have to worry about saying my goodbyes either. I wasn't leaving anyone, or anything, behind. Call it what you want; most call it lonely, but over the years I'd come to learn that being lonely keeps life easy. I kept myself as far from any kind of connection as I possibly could, especially since I knew what it felt like to lose it all.

While most of me was wondering if I'd done the right thing, taking this job, I did also feel a little excitement to get somewhere new. That alone was a feeling I wasn't familiar with. My desire to be anywhere had never been too strong, and I'd never really had all that much to look forward to. There was just something about this drive that flickered the smallest spark of joy in me. Like maybe, after all this time, I was going to find my place—or at least *a* place, a *safe* place.

Loss is tough. Loss, over and over again, everywhere you turn? Well, that will kill you. Damn near killed me, if not by the bombs that took out my unit, then by my own hands here at home. But, as this cruel world would have it, my phone rang and a polite young man on the other end of the phone offered me a job and a place to live. I probably should have turned him down, but the guy sounded like he really did need the help. Besides, it wasn't his fault that I'd changed my mind since I applied. As grumpy as I am, I don't usually pass up on an opportunity to help someone else out. So, rather than letting go of the end of my rope, I found myself right here: southbound to Wrightsville Beach for a new chapter.

Crossing county lines into Wilmington, North Carolina put me about twenty minutes away from the job site, which also happened to serve as my new home. But if I didn't get off this highway and take a leak, I wouldn't make it the rest of the way. I could have made a quick stop on the side of the road, but I figured that public urination wouldn't be a great way to meet anyone in my new town. I drank my weight in sweet tea trying to stay awake on the drive overnight. It was easier now that the sun was up, but my bladder was paying the price.

The gas station seemed to be the go-to place. Though, it might have been because it was the first gas station in fifty miles. I took advantage of the only open parking spot, conveniently next to a beautiful girl in a Jeep, a pair I couldn't ignore.

The doors and the roof had all been removed, and I found myself watching her every move as she turned down her music and rooted through the center console, lifting out a wallet. She jumped to the pavement and my attention shifted quickly to those jeans that fit her some kind of perfect. She had these tall brown leather boots on, and a black tank top that hugged her in all the right places before loosening up and letting go just above her hips. Her long hair, covered in a worn out and torn navy blue hat, was braided down the center of her back.

Now look, in my own defense, I'm not a total pig. I'm polite, and I know that gawking at a girl in the parking lot isn't the sweetest thing to do. But, I'd been alone for a while now. Family, friends, and even pretty girls were foriegn concepts to me these days. So you could say I was glad to have someone that gorgeous to look at, even just for a minute.

After the door closed behind her, I took a moment to shake myself from the trance. Staring at a stranger in a gas station parking lot wasn't my finest moment, and probably wouldn't be a good first impression. I didn't really have an interest in making friends here. My only plans were to work hard, and keep to myself. It was safer that way, for me and for everyone else.

I reached for the door, hopeful to be met with a swift breeze of air conditioning, but instead I was hit with a burning hot splash soaking straight through my shirt, and charring my chest.

"SSSSSSSSHewwwwww" I hissed, jumping back and peeling my shirt away from my skin.

"Oh my gracious." Her voice distracted me. It was the pretty girl. I shouldn't call her that. She obviously had a name. But again, I was so distracted by her that the trance took over, and I just stared. "Oh man, I am so so so sorry. My mom always makes fun of me for getting gas station coffee when she runs a perfectly good cafe. This will give her more to shoot at." She had thrown her hands up to her face. I stepped back to my truck.

"It's alright." I opened the back door and pulled my shirt off, tossing it onto the floor and rooting through my bag for a clean one.

"So... handsome." I heard behind me. I turned to her, smiling, and slipping my arms through my clean shirt. "I mean. Crap. Sorry. I mean, not sorry that you're handsome. Sorry that I said that out loud. Again. Well this is embarrassing."

Her general discomfort was pretty entertaining, nerves or guilt, whichever it was.

"It's okay, really." I said, eyeing her empty hands. I leaned down and picked up the cup she had dropped. "Can I get you a new coffee?" I asked. Come to think of it, she didn't sound like she needed a coffee. If anything I think she'd had a bit too much.

"Uh, I'm pretty sure I should be the one getting you a new coffee. Seeing as how I'm the one who caused this... coffeetastrophe." She waved her hands toward my chest like she couldn't find the words.

"This... what now?"

"I'm sorry, I get funny when I'm nervous. I talk a lot. Well, I talk a lot all the time, but it tends to get a little bit out of control when I'm... well. Like right now." She looked at me blankly for a second. "Ok. So. I'm going to get you a drink. Or whatever it is you came in here for."

"I'm actually just here to use the restroom." I said. She didn't reply, seemingly the first breath she took since she ran into me. Literally. "So you really always talk this much?" I asked, making my way to the bathroom; crazy girl three steps behind me. She was following me, afterall, so maybe the pretty girl was crazy too.

"Only when I'm awake." She said. "Yeah. Well, sorry. I actually have to home. I mean run. Run home. Run errands and then get home. Good Lord, Ruby get it together. So, are you sure I can't get you anything?"

I turned and leaned my back into the bathroom door. "I'm pretty sure I can handle this part. Thanks though." I waved.

"Right. Okay. Well, goodbye then." I heard the door to the bathroom shut behind me. "Sorry about your shirt!" She was hollering through the bathroom door, and I was laughing as quietly as I could. When I came back out, she was gone. Probably a good thing, too. That would have only gotten more awkward.

That wasn't exactly the welcome I had in mind for my first day in a new town. I didn't have anything particular in mind. Actually I just kind of hoped that I could get here, start working, and settle in without making too much of a commotion. Pretty girls to look at wouldn't hurt any.

That part might be nice.

THE ESTATE

THREE

Hobie

There wasn't a single thing about getting to my new job site that felt like the country roads, or the private estate the owner told me about over the phone. If I hadn't been warned ahead of time, I would have thought I had this all wrong. It was looking more like a busy town with a busy life, and less like the heaven on earth I was anticipating. I was trying to get away from all that mess and had high hopes that I'd find some refuge here.

After the gas station, you wind up somewhere around the University. It was the start of fall semester, and I quickly found myself in the hustle and traffic of a college town. But, I recalled the first of many text messages from my new boss.

You'll have to go through the University to get here. Don't worry. They usually keep their noise on that end of town.

Port Dixon was well aware that I was looking to get somewhere quiet. I just wanted a hard day's work, a place to keep my hands busy and my mind quiet. He seemed to understand, and offered me the job almost right away. First impressions, I guess.

Once the University traffic seemed mostly behind me, I started to notice a shift from old beat up cars that I assumed belonged to a bunch of broke college students, to trucks and trailers. Boats, jet skis, and some kind of equipment were being hauled on the back of almost every truck around. Except of course for mine.

I was driving my brother's old Land Cruiser. He bought it from a neighbor in high school, and we spent most of college fixing it up. I think he had intentions of repainting it to polish off all of his hard work, but when Momma passed away we got a bit distracted, and he never got that far. So when I got the keys, I had the rusty pile of metal shined up and repainted a nice dark blue; the last touch it needed to look like the gem I think he wanted it to be.

As I crossed the bridge onto the island, the view started to feel more like the new home I had in mind. There was only a single boat trailer in front of me, and no one behind me. Ervin Road, the last leg to the estate.

Pass the Row, you'll see the cafe on the corner. Pull into the driveway at the office. It's a burgundy cottage with the white flower

25

pots. If Penny isn't out there in the gardens, keep on driving back to the main house.

Another message from the boss, last night. He knew I was hitting the road, and sent a few texts along the way.

I followed the gravel driveway underneath a long strip of live oak trees until I found what I assumed was the main house on the Ervin Estate, certainly not the house that I would be living in.

I was supposed to be moving into a guest house, and Port was pretty clear that it was small and well-loved, but a good place to stay. I definitely wasn't moving into this—the model home for Southern Living. Although, I wasn't disappointed that I'd be spending my time around a place so nice. The house was like something out of the movies. A front porch that wrapped around the house as far as I could see, covered a whole cluster of rocking chairs. The windows were framed in shutters as grand as the house, and probably offered a great view looking out over the magnolia trees that shaded the front side. Port and his wife couldn't be the only ones doing all of this. It looked like the house must have been the pride and joy of the family for quite some time now.

I closed up the doors and noticed the open windows, but decided I'd just let it go. This didn't seem like a place I'd need to lock my doors, or worry about losing my stereo. Just what I needed. The gravel crunched softly under my feet, and other than a few foghorns in the distance, the place seemed pretty quiet. Another one of the boss's notes came to mind as I watched a family step off the front porch and climb into the pickup truck out front. *Step* isn't actually a good way to put it. It was more like they *poured* out of the house, with a steady trail of lunch boxes, soccer balls, a surfboard, and one tired-eyed mom who otherwise looked as if none of the chaos phased her in the least.

Don't worry about the boys, and sorry in advance for any of their mess you run into, trip over, or otherwise find yourself entangled in. They mean well, usually.

I listened to the back and forth of yelling and laughed at the eye roll I figured only a mother could give. Surely, this was Port Dixon's family; his wife and children; twin boys.

"Get in the truck and find a pair of shoes." She said. "You cannot go to school barefoot again." I laughed as I watched her wrangle up the boys, handling the circus like she was used to the madness. She turned to me with an empty exhale as she stepped around to the driver's side door, and waived.

"Hey! You must be Hobie?" she called, hand in the air.

"Yes, ma'am." I answered, removing my cap and returning the wave.

"You can call me Penny. Port's in the kitchen. Go grab some coffee! I'll be back after I get these rascals to school." She was interrupted by one of those rascals leaning out of the drivers side window.

"Can I drive, ma?" he asked, with an innocent grin plastered across his face.

"Can you reach the pedals, Roy?" She stuck her tongue out at him as he groaned in frustration. "Scoot over. Let's boogie."

"Sup, Hobie!" The twins said together, bumping into Penny and making her splash her coffee. They apologized, but it was muffled by their laughter.

She hit the gas and all but peeled off while she called back to me. "Go on in, make yourself at home!" She waved again as they drove away.

I stepped up onto the front porch and turned again to take in the view, feeling a bit of relief. This place had it all, as I expected. I was the newest, poorest, resident on an old money estate property on the water in North Carolina. Whoever designed this porch did it right. Getting a closer look, I saw a swing on either end with a coffee table in front, rocking chairs all over the place, and window boxes full of flowers that matched the pots on the steps. One of those tables already had some dishes out, with glasses and a pitcher of what looked to be fresh iced tea, sweet I was sure. The ceiling was painted that blue everyone in the south likes so much. Maybe this place really was on the cover of a magazine somewhere.

I stepped up to the screen door and rang the bell.

"Hey Hobie, come on in, man!" I heard from the back of the house. I let myself in and roughed my boots on the floor mat at the entry. You could just see the edge of the kitchen from the foyer, so I walked that way, following the sound of dishes clanging.

"Son of a!" I heard him yell, followed by something falling to the floor. "Damn dog." I looked down to see a rottweiler puppy eating up bacon pieces from the kitchen floor.

He stepped around the kitchen island and reached out to me with a handshake, and a frustrated laugh at the dog. "Well, I hope you can make it through the day without bacon. Looks like we're down to biscuits and sweet tea." I laughed and agreed.

"Biscuits will be just fine. Plus, it looks like you just made her day." I knelt down to the puppy who was waddling around lapping up the last of the grease from the tile floor. "Oh, she's just a baby. Look at those paws." The dog reached her paws up to my hands, licking my fingers and gnawing on every part of me she could get to. Definitely a puppy, teeth and all.

"Twelve weeks," Port huffed, hands on his hips. "Twelve weeks of peeing on my carpets, eating my sandwiches, and running through my feet in this kitchen trying to trip me. She's great."

"Ah, I bet everyone loves her." I stood back up to join him.

"That we do." Port leaned back against the countertop and crossed his arms in front of his chest. "So, how was the drive? I hope you didn't have too much trouble through the university. Lot's of good stuff over that way; worth checking out when they're on break and it quiets down a bit over there."

"Well, I just made a quick stop at the gas station on the way in. But, other than that, no, no trouble at all."

29

"Ah!" He raised a finger. "Don't let my mom see you with a cup of gas station coffee. You'll never live it down." Something about that sounded familiar, but I couldn't quite place it.

"Well, you know, the property you've got here is more my style. I'll probably stick around this side of town, if you don't mind." I answered, reaching into a big white bucket with a paw print on the front to grab a few treats for that puppy that was still clawing her way up my jeans. "Here you go—"

"Maggie. It's short for Magnolia. My wife picked that name. The boys thought Magnolia was cheesy, so we went with Maggie to make everyone happy."

"Hey Maggie." I reached back down to give her another scratch between the ears. It was pretty neat to see a Rottweiler with a full tail. She had it wagging so fast it was almost blurry. It brought me a little joy to know that I might get to hang out with this sweet girl every day. That was a new feeling for me; joy.

"Well, hey. Now that you've got the dog wrapped around your finger, maybe she'll spend some time with you and a little less time tripping me in the kitchen." Port continued. "I'm glad you're here. I think you're going to be a big help to us around the estate. I don't really want you working just yet, though. I want you to get in and get settled. Give us all some time to get to know each other a bit. How's that sound to you?"

"Sounds good." In my head, I figured that left room to maybe find a few local restaurants I might like, and of course, unpack. Although, I didn't have all that much to unpack. Every time I moved, I'd gotten rid of more and more stuff I didn't use. For this one, I was down to a large duffel bag full of clothes, and another small bag of odds and ends. I guess a few laid back days before starting my job would be tolerable. I was willing to bet there was plenty around here to do. Couldn't complain about sitting on the sand and wasting time, either.

I followed Port and Maggie who was trotting beside him like her paws were too big for her body. We stepped back out to the front porch, biscuits in hand, and Port poured me a fresh glass of that sweet tea.

"Thank you, sir."

"Oh no way, man. If you're going to work here, you're a friend of ours. You can call me Port, even though officially I may be your boss. All I'm doing is signing a paycheck. We need help and we're lucky to have you. I'll probably end up spending a bit of time working right alongside you, to be honest. Teamwork's pretty big around here."

"Glad to be here, sir. I mean... Port." We started off along the gravel driveway as it continued around the back side of the house. I thought this place was beautiful before, but when we stepped around the home and saw the back of the property, my jaw actually dropped. The driveway pulled around to a backyard that overlooked the marina and the open ocean. A giant rectangular pool took up a large plot of the main cleared land which seemed to lead out toward the barn, and what looked like it might have been the guest house I was moving into.

"I bet the boys love that." I pointed to the pool, which was littered with blow up rafts and noodles, a picture perfect setting for a good family time. I'd always imagined that childhood should look something like this.

"Ah, yes. And they'll appreciate having a new friend to swim with, if you're ever so inclined. Our house is yours, pool and all."

"Thank you. I appreciate that."

"Penny had the boys rushing out for school this morning. She'll be back in a bit. I bet she'll have some sort of treat for us, too. She can't control herself when it comes to that bakery on the other side of the bridge. Some might say they're competition, with the cafe and all. But then again, Miss Linda comes over here for coffee all the time too, so I guess it works out even."

"Sounded like Roy was trying to drive this morning." I joked.

"Wouldn't be the first time." Port laughed. He adjusted his cap and leaned forward onto the fence as we reached the stables. I could tell he was comfortable here. He mentioned that he grew up close by, and it showed. I'd never stayed in one place long enough to know what that felt like.

"Roy and Sam, they're ten. More times than not you'll hear Penny hollerin' their full names. They're trouble makers, you know? They don't have a mean bone in their body, but boy can they whip up some noise and break things. I guess that's what ten year old boys specialize in." He laughed. "Those two scared us right out of having any more kids."

"Well, I'm sure they'll enjoy living here then. Plenty of room to run. Are y'all getting settled?" I asked.

"Not too much to settle, thankfully. We used to live just off the property, so nothing really changed when we moved into this house." He raised his hand, waving across the yard. "We were actually over there, in the house I grew up in—all part of the same property. So it's just unpacking, really. The only thing changing for us is where we lay our heads at night. Penny likes the bigger kitchen too, and I'm not complaining."

A couple horses had been moseying toward us and finally reached the fence. Port gave them a few pats on the nose.

"Climb on up." He said, sitting on the top railing of the fence line. "This is Tigua, and that big butthead over there is Sampson. They're pretty slow nowadays, but they were some wild ones back in their younger years. The boys and my sister are the only ones who ride these guys anymore. My wife and my sister have been talking about making room for a few more — part of the reason we brought you on, actually. Penny is thinking if we can get a better grip on the logistics of the stables, we'll be able to take on another couple of younger horses. They've already got their eyes on a few actually."

"I didn't know your sister lived here too." I said. Port told me about his wife and kids when he hired me, but he hadn't mentioned his sister.

"Well, she doesn't live in the main house. She lived in the guest house until recently, and now she's moving back out to the Row, into the house we grew up in." He pointed toward the cafe.

"Cottage Row is out on the edge of the property, over there. The cafe came first, with a small apartment on top. One by one the houses popped up. First Eddy's place, then my parents. Now it's almost a small neighborhood. It all belongs to us though."

"Well, I don't particularly know how to take care of a horse, but I'm a quick learner." I reached up to Tigua, rubbing his chest. Sampson stepped over, nudging my hand. "Jealous, bud?" I laughed, reaching up to him.

"He's a spirited one, that's for sure. You'll meet my Uncle Eddy sometime today, I'm sure. Sampson picked a fight with Eddy's dad when they first brought him home, and well, the two of them ended up having a special relationship. Sampson won that one, and he's been a cocky butthead ever since." Sampson whinnied at us again and then pushed his nose up against me. Port waved him off, and jumped off the fence. "How about the gardens then. Want to take a look?"

"Lead the way." I followed across the property again, taking in the size of the live oaks. They seemed like the perfect trees for treehouses, or swings. I'd never had anything like that.

We passed a field of hammocks and began walking through a posted, self-guided, garden tour. A welcome sign marked the beginning of the path, and then there were informational signs every so often about the types of flowers found in the area. Sign by sign, we walked through to the other side. Port went through the general ideas for the garden, but said that the ladies would teach me most of what I needed to know.

"Penny and the girls handle most of the garden. So they'll be able to answer any questions you have. Showing you where it is, is about all I'm good for when it comes to this place."

"It's amazing," I said. "Looks well cared for."

"It has been. The estate has been handed down through family for a few generations now. They started the gardens in the sixties, I think. Back then it was just a nice backyard for the family to enjoy, but these days it's become quite the attraction. You'll see a few weddings here in the fall and spring. The Coast Guard usually holds a banque, and a variety of important politicians on the mainland will usually hold some sort of birthday party here each year. The gardens are probably where we have the biggest plans as far as income goes, so I'm sure you'll end up spending a lot of time here. Though, if things go the way Penny plans, we might end up with another person or two working with you. That's a while off yet, though. We're just getting things off the ground for now."

Here and there, I leaned over to rip up a few weeds along the edging as we walked. I was enjoying the scenery, but also getting to know my new boss.

"What was happening here before y'all moved in? It's a family place?" The idea of a property like this one being handed down through family sounded incredible, especially in a small town like this.

"Well, my parents and my uncle have managed the grounds for a while now. They've been taking care of everything and working on ideas for growing the business side of the estate, but Penny and I really want to get to work and bring those ideas to life. Our parents just never had the hands, and it's not a job for just two or three, especially while they were raising the six of us. They're all a bit older now, so we're definitely going to need the help if we're going to keep the place going. Dad and Eddy would prefer to be out on the water every day anyways and well, I think they deserve that. So we're excited to take over, and hopefully see this place grow. I want everyone to be able to experience the beauty of it. I was lucky enough to grow up here. I just want to share that with as many people as we can. It's going to take a lot of work to keep this place running well enough that we can hand it all down one day ourselves."

I never was a particularly sentimental person, but Port's dreams for this place seemed to hold a lot of weight, and a lot of hope. You could tell his heart was in it just by the way he described his home, the way his eyes showed admiration for every little detail. I'd always wished for a place like this, a family like this one. Property or not, it seemed like the generations here were deeply rooted in each other, with families stretching across decades and still managing to stay put and call this place home. It was an idea of belonging that I'd never experienced, but always assumed was out there. I wondered how I might fit in here, or if I ever would.

At the edge of the garden, approaching the house, I heard a rumble and looked up to see Penny coming back up the driveway. In the dust behind her was a Jeep. A familiar looking jeep, actually. No doors, no top. After hearing a rather loud rendition of some late nineties country music, I wasn't surprised at all to catch a better look at the driver.

Now I knew why the Jeep looked familiar; it was. The pretty crazy girl from the gas station was driving. I can't say I was disappointed to get another look at her, and this time I noticed more. She seemed young, younger than me at least. She had sunglasses on now too; black aviators that were entirely too big, but they were still cute. She'd probably look cute in a potato sack, to be honest. Although, I was still caught up in those jeans. She parked next to Penny and jumped out, taking an extra few seconds to look at my truck. I watched her tilt her head like she was trying to figure something out. She was probably wondering where she knew my truck from. Penny offered her a box, and she pulled out a pastry as they walked our way.

"You never fail me." she said, cheersing her pastry to Penny's before we reached them. She stopped chewing when I caught her eye.

"Wow." she mumbled as she shuffled to a stop, reaching up to cover her mouth. Penny slapped her shoulder, and tried to hide her laugh, snort included. "Handsome."

Penny, unable to contain her laughter anymore, hung her head and laughed.

"I mean... ahem. Hello." Ruby coughed, swallowing the rest of her food. "Hi." She tucked her chin down and waived.

Thankfully, before things could get any more awkward, Port interrupted.

"Alright? Uhm. Well, Ruby, this is Hobie Logan. Hobie, my sister Ruby Dixon. She just moved out of the house you'll be taking and back into the house we grew up in. But, like I said, she still spends a lot of time here on the property. When she's not off being rude to new residents and chowing down on sugar bombs."

Ruby turned her cap around backward and stuck her tongue out at Port. She reached out to me, mouth full of the chocolate pastry she had less than gracefully inhaled in one bite, not that it wasn't cute to watch.

"Nice to meet you, Ruby." I shook her hand, and willed myself to let go. I guess I could have mentioned to Port that we had sort of already met. Instead, I followed her lead. She didn't bring it up, so maybe it was better to let that part slide. Ruby had the most beautiful smile I think I'd ever seen. Good thing too, because it distracted me from staring too long at everything else about her. She was definitely going to be off limits. Easy enough. It wasn't really a good idea for me to get involved with anyone anyway.

"Nice to meet you." She mumbled, looking a bit confused, with one hand covering her full mouth. "Can't get in between me and my breakfast." She laughed, turning a bright shade of strawberry. "Or my coffee."

"What's on the docket today, Ruby?" Penny asked her as we walked closer to the house.

"Oh! Is dad here?" Ruby stepped up onto the porch and made her way to the door, looking back at me before she stumbled into the doorframe. I followed the crowd inside, and tried to pretend I didn't notice. She sure did know how to boost a guy's ego, though. I'd have more than enough entertainment around here if she kept on staring at me like that.

"They took the boat out around four this morning. I'd bet they'll be back in time for lunch. What's up?" Port sat down at the kitchen island and picked his own pastry out of the box. "Miss Linda is going to kill me with all this sugar." He pushed the box toward me. "Trust me. Worth the calories." He added.

"I need to borrow dad's drill." Ruby continued.

"Ah, it's just out in the barn. I'll go grab it." Port got up to walk outside, but stopped and turned around. "Wait a second." Hands on his hips. "What did you do? What are you fixing?"

"Have some faith, brother man." I liked her attitude, and the obvious quality sibling relationship. "Ryan and Lucas sent over a few new photos. I picked up the prints this morning—" She stopped just long enough to glance my way, and I began to put her morning together a piece at a time as she continued. "Anyway, they're all framed up and ready to hang in the cafe. I'm rearranging one of the gallery walls to make some space and need a drill." She stuck her tongue out at him like she had before, which was a face I was already beginning to enjoy. He smiled and returned the glare as she came back to the coffee pot. "I'm going to make some fresh coffee. Anyone want some?"

"Thanks, I've already had plenty this morning." I said. Okay, so maybe that was rude, but mostly I found it funny. Her eyes widened and she did her best, although useless, to hide a smile.

"I feel like this is a great time to remind you that it would be wise to cut back on your caffeine intake." I cleared my throat in attempts to avoid laughing at Port, and the ease with which he picked on his sister. "Just go ahead and make a full pot. I could use it. I'll be right back." He stepped out onto the porch, leaving me in the kitchen with Penny and Ruby.

"Penny, your property is incredible. Thanks for giving me the opportunity here." Ruby turned around and looked as though she'd figured me out, or was at least a little more intrigued.

"Oh, right, the new ranch handsome." Ruby stuttered. "*Hand*. Ranch hand. *Shit*."

"Well, it's not a ranch, Ruby. So no..." Penny looked between us, confused. "But yes, Hobie is going to be helping us out, and staying in the guest house. Weren't you listening to anything your brother said outside? Hopefully we can get ahead on the work that needs to be done around here. At the very least, maybe we can get into some sort of routine."

"With a little time, ma'am, I'm sure I can help you get this place into shape. I hope you'll find things easier down the road." I said.

"Ohhh, maybe Port will let us get more horses then." Ruby added.

"I doubt it, but we'll see. Let's get on top of the mess we already have." She turned to the cabinet and pulled out a few mugs. "How do you take your coffee, Hobie?"

"Black, ma'am."

Ruby snorted as she laughed. "Ma'am. Sheesh. Y'all really act your age sometimes."

"Can it, Ruby." Penny rolled her eyes and looked back to me. "It's just Penny, seriously. We're all family around here. Relax." I nodded, sipping my coffee.

"That's disgusting." Ruby said as she poured what seemed like a half gallon of creamer into her coffee. "Black coffee is like tar. I don't know how you can drink that."

"Ruby! What is with you this morning?" Penny was still looking back and forth between us, and I struggled not to speak up and explain our encounter from earlier. "Here's an idea. Why don't you take Hobie down to the cafe? Introduce him to your parents, and see if you can find my dad, while you're at it. I bet he'll hang those prints for you." She looked back and handed me a lid for the coffee cup.

"Okay seriously, have I not complained enough about how wasteful y'all are? I'm just going to order you the tumblers and get rid of all this plastic junk you insist on using. Your coffee will taste better too, you know." Ruby grunted, and stepped to the door.

"Okay, alright, miss environmentally friendly. I'm sorry. Help me save the Earth."

"I will." Ruby snapped.

"No work yet, Hobie. Just get to know everyone and get settled. We'll just ease into things here, okay? I thought I'd take you into town today too, if you're up for it. The kitchen in your house isn't huge, and you're welcome to share meals with us. But I wanted to make sure you have everything you need.

"Thank you, that sounds great." I wouldn't mind having meals with the family now and then, but I also intended to keep my own stash of snacks and beer too. I was pretty used to alone time.

"Alright, then!" Ruby jumped down from the counter. "Shall we?"

"Yes ma'am." I said, following her out the door.

"Yeah, we're gonna work on those ma'ams. They might be old, but I'm not."

"You're not?" I asked. She looked at me like she was disgusted that I'd asked.

"Absolutely not. I'm twenty two."

"Oh. Definitely not into ma'am territory yet." I said.

"Absolutely not." She was feisty, and I liked it.

"Sorry, then. Guess I'll stick with Ruby." I smiled, but she wasn't looking my way to notice. Instead I was following just behind her, keeping my eyes on the view of those blue jeans. A view that was getting better by the minute, and harder to ignore.

We got across the property to what I assumed was Cottage Row. The cafe was on the corner right by the entrance to the property, and neighboring houses lined the street, with empty land nearby.

"Hey baby doll!" I heard as we stepped into the cafe. Over the threshold, I was hit with a wave of heaven—a smell made up of fresh coffee, hot breakfast, and just a little bit of whatever God blessed perfume Ruby had on.

"Hey, Momma. This is Hobie. Hobie, this is Momma." I shook her hand and then turned to hear the banter back at the door.

"Nice to meet you, ma'am." I said.

"Goodness, sweetheart, call me Amy. Or, momma. Up to you. I answer to both." She said, going back to the counter.

Ruby continued. "And those two fools over there are my Dad, Rhett, and my Uncle Eddy; that's Penny's dad." The men were bickering back and forth.

"Hang on, now. Port and Penny, y'all are cousins?" Suddenly I was a bit concerned with regards to my bosses'... marital affairs, genetically speaking.

"Haha, no. Not exactly." Ruby laughed, and for just a second, for the first time in a long time, I caught enough of a breath that I started to relax. "But we were basically raised that way."

"Hobie! Nice to meet you, son. I'd like you to know that I caught the bigger trout this morning, and Eddy here owes me a beer." Rhett shook my hand and then walked behind the counter, kissing Amy on the cheek.

"You're full of crap," Eddy retorted with an eye roll as he sat down next to Ruby at the bar.

"Hey, sweetheart." He kissed her head as he walked by. "What are you doing today?"

"I've got the rest of these prints ready to sell. Can y'all quit your bickering about the fish and help me hang them up?" She pointed back and forth between the two of them.

"Sure. Weather's supposed to be beautiful this weekend. I'll bet you sell quite a few. We should get a nice burst of visitors over the next few days."

I spent the next half hour or so listening to Ruby babble on and on all about the cafe and Cottage Row, including the house that she was moving into now. Or, moving back into. It sounded like Rhett and Amy raised their kids in one house and Eddy raised his kids in another. The parents had all recently moved into the new, smaller houses on the estate, leaving their childhood homes up for grabs. Ruby seemed excited about the idea, and talked about drawing up plans for remodeling the kitchen in a way that kept it's charm.

After a while, Rhett and Eddy took off and I listened as Ruby told Amy all about how the three of them were the new "squad".

"What squad?" I asked.

Ruby cackled and Amy rolled her eyes.

"We used to call the old ladies in town the *broad squad*. They could bicker and gossip all day long, and still have enough to talk about on the phone later at night. Ruby here seems to think that we're old enough now to take over the title. Which I strongly disagree with, I might add. We're just older. We're not archaic." Ruby met Amy's scowl with a stuck out tongue. The family seemed to pick on eachother, and the dynamic they shared was something I admired already.

"Well, Hobie, we're glad to meet you. Let me know if there's anything I can do to help you get settled. Obviously I am always good for a fresh cup of coffee and something to eat." She patted my shoulder and walked back behind the counter as another group walked into the cafe.

"So..." Ruby started. "Want to go see your new home?"

"Your old one?" I asked. "Just making sure I have this all right."

"That's right. But, I'm completely moved out. All yours. No worries. I mean some of my things are still in there, like some furniture and kitchen stuff, but I was planning on leaving those anyway. If there's anything I need I'll let you know. Come on, then. I'll help you get in and settled."

"Thanks. Just maybe not dump this coffee on me." I gestured at the full cup in her hands. "I don't have all that many clean shirts with me. So maybe we can just not make that a habit." I joked.

"No promises. I do make a mean pot of coffee though. Maybe you can have your morning coffee with me and let me practice on you." She closed her eyes and reached up a finger, correcting herself. "Practice not spilling coffee on you, I mean."

"How much coffee do you drink in a day?" I asked.

She answered me with a glare, the kind that seemed to say *don't you dare question my coffee intake.*

"Coffee sounds good." Something about her already had me loosened up. She was easy to talk to and I found myself being sarcastic with her. I couldn't remember the last time I felt like that with anyone. Maybe it was our abrasive first encounter, or maybe it was how cute she was. Although, she was still off limits.

I spent the rest of that day getting toted around the property and the rest of the island. Ruby showed me most everything else at the estate, and then Penny took me into town to make sure I'd had everything I needed for the house, including another pit stop by Linda's bakery for a fresh box of treats.

I passed out relatively early that night, mostly because I was tired from the drive. It was also dark and quiet, which I liked. It seemed like I might actually get some peaceful sleep here, which is exactly what I was looking for.

In search of a new routine and good habits, I started out the next morning with a run, exploring the closest edges of town. I had breakfast on my own, took a quick trip back into town just to explore, and then came back for a quiet night at the house. After a walk down around the marina, I settled back in the living room and opened my computer. Naturally, the internet was password locked. I didn't want to interrupt Port, since they were out doing some family dinner thing with the kids. So, I figured I would ask Ruby. I didn't need to look for a reason to go see her, but needing the internet password seemed harmless.

FOUR

Ruby

Maybe God has a bigger plan for me than I had for myself. Like this journey never ends.

There was no other movie on earth that drove me crazy, broke my heart, and made me smile quite like *A Walk To Remember*. It didn't hurt that Landon Carter was easy on the eyes. I could have looked at that boy for days on end. Regardless, the love story? *Swoon.* I'd watched it so many times that I could recite the entire movie, word for word. I didn't even need to be watching it. I could literally spit it out start to finish, all from memory.

The knocks at the door interrupted the holy grail of movies, and had me irrationally frustrated. Not that I was going to miss anything new, but seriously, interrupting the greatest movie of all time? The audacity. I let it slide pretty fast though when I opened the door and saw who was on the other side.

That sort of tall, dark, and handsome could be forgiven of a whole lot. Throw in the large muscles, and the couple days of scruff on a jawline that looked like it was carved straight from ice, and I'd have let just about anything slide, truthfully. Come to think of it, I was ready to be a willing participant in whatever it was that needed forgiving in the first place.

"Hey." Hobie was... simple. Monotonous. Not unkind, just, seemed like he was bored before I even said a word.

"Hey there." I instantly regretted my—afternoon watching a movie on the couch with a bowl full of french vanilla ice cream—outfit. I was confident that I looked like a homeless person. Better yet, a homeless looking hopeless romantic who probably had gobs of mascara running down her cheeks from sobbing at all the dreadfully happy moments of young and perfect love in this movie. The movie that I loved until right this very second. The movie that I now regretted choosing today. Actually, that's not true. I never regretted watching this movie. I just regretted letting Hobie in to see that I was watching it, and that I was clearly very distraught about the life and trials of Landon Carter and Jamie Sullivan. Even their names were perfect.

"Did he just propose to her?" Hobie asked. I realized that I hadn't actually paused the movie. I left him at the door while I ran for the remote to try again. Turning back around, I saw that he hadn't moved, and was just smiling at me from the porch.

"You can come in, you know. Do you want a drink? Water or something? I've got fresh tea but, I should warn you. It's sweet."

"I'm alright, thanks. So, did he?"

"Did who what?" I asked, thoroughly confused.

"That guy. He just asked her to marry him?" He stood there, halfway between the television and the kitchen, with his hands in his pockets. Still monotonous. Still handsome as all get out.

"Oh. Landon. Yes. He did. Why?"

"She looks twelve." Still monotonous, but this time with a hint of sarcasm.

"Well, I think she's actually like, seventeen. But... wait. Why'd you stop by? Certainly it wasn't to stand here and criticize my favorite movie." Being drop dead gorgeous didn't give him the right to attack Landon Carter. No one criticizes Landon Rollins Carter.

"Oh. Right. I'm having trouble getting onto the internet over at the house, but it looks like everythings all set up. I was wondering if I could just get the password from you."

"Oh, yes. Of course. Let me get a pen and paper real quick so I can write it down for you." Shit. *Shit*. I was about to embarrass myself even more.

"Imightkissyouimightbebadatit" He read the password as if it was actually just one long word. He stopped to think and then looked up at me smiling.

"It's a quote from th— you know what don't make fun of me. You have the key to the world wide web. Just say thank you and stop trash talking the greatest movie ever made." As usual, with my rising temper, came my faster rate of speech. Louder too, with matching hand gestures. "Broaden your horizons a bit. Maybe a sweet love story would do you some good. The world would be a better place, you know, if everyone could just appreciate a good romance." I rattled all of that off faster than I could take a breath. He made me nervous.

"Thank you, Ruby." He held the notecard up. "I appreciate it. Maybe once I get the internet working, I'll look up this movie of yours." He nodded and smiled before he stepped back through the front door.

"Enjoy." I closed and locked up behind him and watched through the window as he walked back across the property to his house. When he stepped up onto his front porch, it occurred to me how long I had been watching him, floating on that line between watching and stalking. I couldn't help it. It was easy to stare at a man with arms like that, all big and strong.

I turned back to the television, grabbed the remote and pressed play. After I plopped back down on the couch, equal parts irritated that he interrupted and bummed that he didn't stay longer, it occurred to me that I'd been worried about what I looked like. Hobie likely just saw me at my worst. I ran over to the bottom of the stairwell and looked in the mirror, and my reflection confirmed it.

"Oh dang it!" I huffed out loud as I wiped some of the mascara from underneath my eyes. I was not making a good impression with the new town stud. I was going to have to work on that. Hobie: two. Ruby: zip.

The next morning, I woke up early in hopes of surfing on my own a bit before my lessons started. Climbing up into the Jeep, I spotted Hobie jogging my way. He had a shirt on, but it was fitted, so he really may as well not have. Anything that could have been left to the imagination was neatly outlined by the sweat soaking through, just making me wish even more that the shirt was off completely. I felt tacky, watching him like that. I shouldn't be wishing the new guy was running around all naked. Not that I'd complain. I mean, not that I'd really have anything to compare him to.

Okay well that's not true either. I had guy friends, and I'd dated here and there. I just hadn't really spent too much time with guys who were less than dressed. Well, it is the beach afterall, so I guess you could say I was used to guys running around in swim trunks. I mean it's more abnormal around here for people to be fully clothed than not. But that's not the point. I wasn't here imagining him in swim trunks. I was here pleading with the hot guy gods to see this man naked as can be. I mean, I'm just saying, if he decided to run around in a bit less clothing than he currently had on, well, I wouldn't complain.

I snapped back to fake meddling in my car to make certain that he didn't catch me staring as he got closer to the property. At the edge of my driveway, he removed his headphones and slowed to a walk, giving me an opportunity to stare too long again. I ran my fingers through my hair and took a quick swipe under my eyes to catch any makeup remnants from yesterday.

"Morning," he huffed.

"Morning, Hobie. How are you?" I asked, realizing that I was putting forth a genuine effort to play it cool.

"Tired. A bit sore. Trying to find a good route for morning runs. Any advice?" He kept his hands on his hips as he caught his breath.

"Well, I can't run. I mean I can... I will. I just don't really like to run around town. I'd rather surf. Or swim. Water based activities are all the workouts I really care for. Except playing with the boys. That's definitely a work out. If I could bottle up the energy of ten year old twins and sell it I'd probably make a fortune."

"Right. Well, then." He went to put a headphone back into his ear. All that talking and I still hadn't answered his question, typical actually. Add some handsome distraction and I'm about as useless as decaf coffee.

"Oh, well. I mean I can still make a few suggestions. Stay away from the Marvin house. Theodore is as old as can be, and doesn't like anyone on his property. If you even run by there you risk a five minute lecture on how close is too close to his grass. And he won't remember it so he'll do the same thing again the next time you run by. He actually brought a map over to Port once, and offered other routes for him to stay away from his house. There's a nice path that goes from the island all the way to the University. It's pretty full of students but they'll generally stay out of your way. Except for the poodle at the Ladham's house. He's jumped the fence a few times. Not too fond of people, that one. But if you just run past the house really fast and don't make eye contact, he might ignore you. It's the lingering that's dangerous. And then of course, on the weekends or during breaks, the campus can be a really nice place to go. Especially if you like to look at a lot of really charming architecture. The school has managed to keep a lot of the old age and small town charm. And if you like that, you might be interested in checking out other beautiful towns on the water, Beaufort in particular. It's one of my favorites."

"Okay." He said.

"I'm sorry, are you always so quiet? Have I said something wrong? I mean I know that the coffee spill wasn't exactly my finest moment, not for first impressions or anything. But..."

"No, I'm just a good listener." He smiled. "Seems like that's going to work out well for me."

"Was that an insult? Because if that was an insult then, you know, I just have to—"

"No. I just meant... balance. That's all." He put his headphones back into his ears and took a few steps backward. "See you later, Ruby."

No one had to remind me that I was an extrovert. I spoke fast, and I spoke my mind. Always have. You have to be loud and quick if you want to keep up in a family with five other kids. I'm a product of my environment.

Hobie just seemed like he didn't know what to do with that. My whole family was rather social and talked *a lot*. So in all fairness, I didn't really know what to do with anyone who couldn't keep up. Maybe he was just shy, starting out a new job and moving to a new town. Or, maybe he was actually not interested in a friendship of any kind. He was always polite, but he didn't seem eager to chat. Not that we needed to talk all the time, but gracious. A bit boring, that one. Maybe he just needed to warm up. In all fairness, I could have given him a little more time, and a little less fire.

Tower twelve was the home of the breakfast club—not the movie—but the informally gathered surf club. It wasn't a well known or easily accessible spot to tourists, so for the most part it was easy to share the water. I stretched and wrapped the leash around my leg, still thinking about my encounter with Hobie earlier that morning. He was as hard to talk to as he was easy to look at. I almost took it as a personal challenge to get him to warm up to us and get comfortable. Maybe he would enjoy surfing.

I found the boys pretty quickly. Sam and Roy were known to skip school to go surfing on a good morning. I was glad to see them here on a Saturday, and know that they wouldn't get in trouble for spending the morning in the water.

"Hey Aunt Ruby!" Roy called. A few arms popped up out of the water as I paddled out. All the usuals, which was a welcome sight.

"Alright boys." I rubbed my hands together like I was excited. "Best wave this morning gets out of the dishes at dinner."

"That's not fair. We always end up stuck with dishes anyway while you grown ups have your drinks and talk on the porch." Sam rolled his eyes and even used his fingers for air quotes around "grown ups". His teenage years were going to be wild.

"Not tonight, scout's honor. If I lose, I'll do dishes, all by myself."

"Or you could invite the new guy over, and he can help you." I recognized that voice. I turned around to find my Aunt Allison in the lineup.

"Why would I do that?" I asked, blushing.

"Ohhhhhh " The boys started. "Ruby and Hobie sitting in a tree. K I S S I—"

"Oh for the love—catch a wave and get out of here with your nonsense." I sliced my hand through the surface to send a spray across the boys.

They paddled back over to their friends and I sat on my board next to Allison.

"Y'all could at least give him a full week to get settled before you get to work on pawning him off. You don't even know if he's single. And who even said I was looking?"

"Oh please. I saw the way that boy looked at you. For your own sake, I hope he's single. He's interested; I can see it in his eyes. And of course you're looking, so don't pretend you're not. You haven't so much as even kissed a boy in at least a year, and I'm pretty sure the last time was thanks to the alcohol in your system and not an actual relationship." Sometimes I felt like my chatter-box ways actually came from her.

"What are you talking about? I've dated."

"No, Ruby. You've gone on dates here and there, first dates. And you broke things off early with what's his name when he got frisky on the promenade. So, yes, I do think you're at least... available. Besides, if you haven't been looking, I'll just go ahead and clue you in; that man is all sorts of good looking. And if I was your age, honey—"

"Alright, alright. So I'm embarrassingly single. We don't need to proclaim that all over town. And I didn't ditch him for being frisky. I ditched George because I wasn't interested in being frisky *with him*. I'm not a prude, I just haven't... found the right guy. Yet."

Allison just laughed and let it go. Although, I knew her well enough to know that she wouldn't really be letting it go any time soon. "Ahhh here's a good one. Let's ride."

FIVE

Hobie

Port mentioned that they were having everyone over for dinner tonight, and suggested I join them. But I was so tired from my first few days working on the property that I didn't feel up to going; not physically or socially. I hadn't gotten into much of a routine yet, but I'd made good headway into the list of things Port needed to be fixed, moved, or otherwise tended to.

To be honest, I didn't think I was going to feel up to a dinner like that, regardless of my energy level. I was never one for large crowds. As much as I'd enjoy hanging out with Port, he made it pretty clear that a family dinner around here was more like a block party. Judging by the activity and the noise level I was getting from my front window, I'd say block party was an understatement.

Instead, I stepped out onto the front porch with my own dinner, and sat down to watch from a distance. I had fixed myself a plate full of my usual simple dinner: cooked carrots and broccoli, with a cup full of baked beans. I stuck to a pretty basic diet. I ate fruits, vegetables, eggs, and beans, with a steak or two thrown in for good measure. After you spend a few deployments overseas, you find a whole new appreciation for fresh food, and I came home with a particular hankering for produce. I figured moving to Wrightsville would also offer me an opportunity to expand my palate for seafood. It sounded like Rhett and Eddy would be good teachers.

I was distracted when I saw, or heard, rather, Ruby pull up to the house. Seemed that she always had some sort of noise roaring through her speakers, and she was usually screaming right along. I'd say singing, but I don't think you could actually call that singing. I was kind of impressed that her speakers weren't blown. She must have had a quality sound system. She jumped out of the jeep and waved before looking back and forth to the party at the house.

Don't. I thought. *Don't come over here.*

She was gorgeous and funny. She talked a lot, but not in an annoying way. It was more like she just talked enough that I didn't have to—and I didn't mind listening. She was easy to enjoy, but that was exactly the problem.

I needed her to walk away and continue on over to the big house. I'd barely been here one week and I was already more attracted to her than I had ever been to anyone else in my life. It was the kind of attraction that had me wanting to be closer to her. I didn't want to just work with her, I wanted to be friends. In all honesty I wanted to be the kind of friend who gets all the benefits. Those kinds of benefits were not on the list of possibilities when she was the boss' little sister, and technically a coworker. And technically... well she was twenty two. Legal, but she was certainly way too young for me, at my own ripe old age of thirty three.

I cleaned my plate and set it down on the table as Ruby stepped up onto the front porch, sitting right down in the chair next to me. She sure was comfortable around me already.

"So, how was your weekend, and your first few days here at the circus?" she asked, kicking her feet up onto the railing. It caught me off guard, the way that she just showed up and made herself at home. Not that it bothered me, I kind of liked it.

"Weekend was nice. Work was nice. I think I'll like it around here. Quiet. Plenty to do here at the house too, now that I have the internet set up. Thanks for that." A mix of guilt and embarrassment crossed her face.

"Sorry I yelled at you. I was..." She waved her hands like she couldn't find the words. "Well. I'm sorry."

"Like I was saying," I smiled to ease the mood. "Everything here seems nice and quiet, which is all I was really hoping for."

"Nice and quiet, yes. Of course, only if the boys are in school. Just wait until this summer when they're here every day burning things down." She laughed, though it sounded a bit stressed.

"They can't be that bad," I said. "They seem like cute kids."

"Ha!" She cackled. "Royal and Sampson Dixon are the furthest things from cute kids you could possibly get."

"Wait, Royal?" I asked. "Which one is that?"

"Royal and Sampson, family names. They go by Sam and Roy. Especially Sam. Don't let him hear you call him Sampson. He hates sharing a name with a horse."

"That does kind of suck." I said.

"Yeah. I don't think anyone really thought about that when the boys were born. Anyway... Roy is the one with the longer hair that never looks brushed, usually because it isn't. Usually he's still dripping saltwater. Sam has shorter hair. Otherwise, they're identical. Not a single thing alike when it comes to personality though."

"Ah, okay. Roy and Sam. So, they spend most of their time surfing then? I've seen them race off with their boards in the mornings."

"They do. Roy more so. He wants to follow mom's footsteps, being the surf champ and all. That little grom can't keep his toes dry. He's placed in more competitions than mom ever even entered, and they're only ten." She turned to face me, and I had to look away. Her sky blue eyes could have possessed me to do just about anything.

"Does your mom still surf?"

"No," Her shy laugh caught my attention. "No. Mom used to surf a lot more. I think when she took over the cafe, she

60

kind of put surfing on the backburner. Still goes out now and then, but dad says it doesn't seem to bring her the same kind of happiness that it used to."

It seemed like a touchy subject, and I knew about those all too well.

"Do you surf?"she asked.

"Never tried." I kept my eyes forward on the party.

"Well, I'm sure you'll learn, living here. I'll teach you if you want. There's nothing like it. I've got a free spot on Tuesday and Thursday evenings, if you want it. Just say the word and I'll put you on my schedule."

"Your schedule?" I laid my hands over my waist and propped my feet up on the railing like she did, trying to force myself to relax.

"Yep. It's one of my many adventures." She laughed. "I sell those prints of the boys' photography at the cafe, I work behind the counter a few mornings a week, and teach surf lessons in the evenings as long as the weather stays in check."

"Sounds like you keep busy."

"Just busy enough to keep things fun. I've never really been one for wasting time. Speaking of, why are you sitting here eating? Dinner's over there." She stood up and pointed to the house. "You coming? Dad and Eddy usually have some sort of fresh catch on the grill. If nothing else, the boys will bring a few buckets of shrimp back from the boat. And the girls will be over in a while with a better supply of alcohol. Although, there's no shortage to begin with. I'm sure you could find something you'd like over there."

I stood up and grabbed my plate and beer. "I'm going to pass tonight, actually. Have fun though." I nodded as I backed toward the screen door, leaning my way back into the house.

"Alright. Your loss! Every Saturday night though, rain or shine. You can pretty much count on the whole town being over here. Food's good. Company's better. Wouldn't miss it if I were you." She stepped down off the porch and turned back to face me. "Let me know if you change your mind." She waved and turned to walk on.

It sounded like fun, really. But I hadn't been in a group that size since... well, in a few years. For a long time now, I'd preferred keeping things simple, and keeping to myself. Then I somehow found myself here, surrounded by a family that never stopped talking and never stopped moving.

Stepping inside, I noticed it again; my house smelled like her. It was everywhere. The furniture, the bedroom, it all smelled like Ruby—and I didn't hate it. I watched her walk over to the big house as I washed my dishes and set them on the drying rack. I swapped my laundry and put away what was clean. I was wiping down the kitchen counters when I heard the most god awful scream coming from outside.

I dropped the dish rag, and ran out onto the front porch just in time to see Roy and Sam leading a small cluster of kids right in my direction, with a football in the air between them. Alright, so it was a good scream, though it sounded like death. I was going to learn a bit more about kids living here, at least these kids.

The boys settled in the open area in front of the guest houses and began what I assumed to be a game of catch, though I quickly learned it was actually full on tackle football. It wasn't even a full minute before one of the boys stood up from the first hit with a bloody nose. After a quick swipe on his sweatshirt sleeve, they all just continued playing. *Kids.* I laughed. Maybe Ruby was right. Guess I'd have to keep an eye on these two. Or, eleven, it seemed.

Sam saw me on the porch and waved, heading my way.

"Hey Sam, how's it going?" I leaned on my elbows on the porch railing and watched as he stepped up across the yard.

"Hey Mr. Hobie. Want to play football?"

"Nah buddy, I'll just watch. Y'all are pretty good. Maybe take it easy on the face shots though. How's his nose?" I nodded back out to the game and Sam climbed up to sit on the porch railing.

"Oh, that's Ryan Gillmore. He goes by Gills. He and Roy are pretty rough. One of them is always cut up and bleeding. Don't worry about them."

"You take it a bit easier on the physical violence, then?" I asked.

"Yeah. I prefer not to be covered in blood. I get my fair share from soccer and all, but those two, they're just buck wild. Makes mom crazy. I've lost count of how many times Roy has been to the hospital for stitches. Dr. Malone told him next time he comes in bleeding, he's going to teach him how to stitch up his own wounds. Mom said that sounded like good savings at the emergency room."

"Dr. Malone sounds like a cool dude."

"He is. He's pretty good friends with my dad. I'm sure he'll be around soon, if he isn't at dinner already." Sam looked at me like he wanted to ask me something.

"What is it, buddy?"

"Well, are you coming over for dinner? I haven't seen you hang out with anyone. Do you have friends here? You could bring them too, you know. Mom always gets excited when someone new shows up."

Kids didn't miss a beat, that was for sure. I figured honesty was the best way to go, although he was pretty young. So, I thought I'd keep it simple.

"Nah bud, just me. I'm not from around here. You seem pretty cool, maybe I'll just hang out with you." I joked. Although, he did seem like a pretty cool kid. Wild as they were together, Sam seemed like a little bit of an outsider.

"I'm sorry you're here by yourself, Mr. Hobie." He had hung his head as he answered.

"That's alright. I think I'll be just fine. I'll tell you what. Why don't you go play football with your friends. I want to see what kind of arm you're working with here." I jostled his shoulder just a bit.

"I'm not really working with any kind of arms. I'm more of a foot guy. I play soccer! I have a game this week in Maryland. I

64

think Aunt Ruby might be taking me up there, actually. You should come."

"Well, thanks for the invite. I'll talk to Ruby, okay?" He reached up for a high five on his way back down to the grass. "Go on, then. I'll see you later." He waved as he jogged back toward the other kids and jumped up to intercept one of their tosses. I polished off my beer and made my way back inside, wondering what that must feel like. This kid grew up in an incredible home, with a perfect family, and has probably never spent a moment alone in his whole ten years. No wonder he noticed that I kept to myself. He probably didn't understand the idea of it. Lucky kid.

The boys continued playing as Eddy and another man walked up to the porch. For the large property that was supposed to be quiet and peaceful, it sure felt like round robin here with the constant visitors. Fitting though, since that's presumably what front porches are for anyway.

"Hey Eddy." I shook his hand, and reached out for the other. "Sir." He shook my hand with a warm smile. He was much younger than Eddy, likely closer to my age, but the two seemed close.

"Hey Hobie, this is Jack. He's a good friend of ours. You'll probably see him around, at least at dinner each week. He helps with school carpool some days too."

"Jack Sollerton." He introduced himself with another handshake. "I hear Port brought you on to help with the property."

"Yes, sir." I answered. "Did y'all come to watch the boys play?"

"Oh, no." Jack reached into his pocket and pulled out a small bottle. "My son ran off with his friends before I remembered to give him his medicine." He threw a hand up over his eyes, blocking the sun, as he peered into the crowd of players. "Reed!"

One of the kids called a timeout, and jogged over to us at the porch.

"Hey dad! 'Sup, Eddy?" The boy, Reed, fist bumped them both before his dad playfully punched his shoulder.

"Dude. Manners." Jack pointed to me.

"'Sup?" He reached a fist out to me.

"Dude! More manners." Jack added.

"Sorry," Reed groaned and rolled his eyes. "'Sup, *sir*?"

I laughed and popped my knuckles to his. "Hey, Reed. I'm Hobie."

"Hey, Hobie." He turned back to his dad, eyeing the medicine bottle held out to him. "Dad, can it wait? I thought I'd just take it before bed. It makes me feel so tired."

"Sorry bud. You know the rules." Jack opened the bottle and Eddy handed him a bottle of water. Reed took two of the pills and handed the water back to Eddy.

"Thanks, Eddy." Reed shrugged and took off back toward his friends and the football.

"Kids." Jack huffed.

"Alright, man." Eddy turned back to me. "That's all we were after. You coming over for dinner? Grill's hot."

"Oh, uhm... sorry, not tonight. I have a few things to do around here."

"Alrighty then. See you tomorrow." Eddy didn't pester, and I appreciated it.

"Nice to meet you, Jack." I shook his hand and nodded as they walked away.

I stepped back inside then in hopes of avoiding any more visitors for the night.

The next morning, I walked over to the stables to find Ruby on the fence, handing carrot sticks to the horses. I took myself through the reminder that I had basically memorized: *she's the boss's sister. She'll only get hurt. She's better off without you.*

It was going to take a serious effort on my part, keeping my eyes off of her, and my head out of the gutter. Not that thinking about a girl was automatically in the gutter, but it certainly wasn't appropriate for now.

She had on another tight and dark pair of blue jeans that only helped her already perfect figure, the same tall brown leather boots that came up over her calves, and a black tank top. She had her hair done in two long braids, falling out of that same ball cap. It seemed she had a uniform, a rather simple style, and it was a good one.

"Morning, Ruby." I stepped up next to her and watched as she fed the horses. "Is this breakfast?"

"No," she laughed. "Just a little extra spoiling. They like carrots, so I try to bring them a good snack whenever I come over. As long as they're nice, right buddy?" She held another carrot out to Tigua, and Sampson came up to join them, almost knocking right into Ruby. "Easy slugger," she said. "There's plenty, you pig."

"So, what are we doing after snack time?" I tried to shift my attention from the girl to the horse.

"Well, I figured I'd show you what a typical morning looks like in the stables. Obviously, it's Sunday, and we don't expect you to be working seven days a week. But I'm here if you'd like to join me."

"I would." I answered. "The days don't really bother me. If it needs to get done, I'm happy to do it."

Her smile had me staring again, as she paused, seeming like she couldn't find her next words. She cleared her throat and abruptly continued.

"We need to start looking at clearing out the other stalls, and work on really getting this place ready. I want to make room for some new rescues. There's a couple getting pulled off the tracks in Louisville sometime this winter. At least, that's what the rumors are. But, Port won't let me bring them in until I have things in order here. He has a point. Problem is, I can't do it all on my own. That's where you come in. You know, muscles and brawn."

She wasn't going to make it easy on me. I know she didn't mean anything by it, the way she grabbed my arm while she was cracking a joke about my muscles. Maybe she wasn't trying to flirt, but it sure was hard to ignore. I kept my smile tucked away as I answered. "Well, whatever you need, just let me know."

Her eyes lingered on mine for just a blink too long, before she jumped down to the ground, adjusting her hat. "Well, let's get started then."

We spent a few hours going through the basics of how to take care of the stables. We filled buckets with their food for the next few days, cleaned out the stalls and laid new straw, refilled their water, brushed them down, swept up the stable floor and then spent another few minutes cleaning up the field while the horses walked around and messed with a few toys. I was surprised to learn that the horses could sort of kick a ball. After we finished, she opened up a gate on the far end of the stables and we watched as they walked off into another field. Well, Ruby watched the horses. I watched Ruby.

"So, who did all of this work before you? Before I came here?"

"Until you got here, it was mostly just me and Penny. Mom helps now and then, but it's not really her favorite thing. She likes the horses, but not that much. I guess before Penny it was mom and Nori, and I guess they probably learned from Jane and Dana. I think Nori did most of the work though. Mom just fed them, and rode them. She's not one for hard work." Ruby laughed, brushing her hands off on her blue jeans, drawing my attention straight back to her hips. "She likes her air conditioned coffee shop, dirt free and pretty."

"Where's Nori? Have I met her?" It would have been easy to miss a whole person in this place, there sure were enough of them running around.

She inhaled slowly, as the joy fell from her face. "My Aunt Nori," she started. "She was Uncle Eddy's wife. She passed away when we were little. I was really young. It's just been Momma, Daddy, and Uncle Eddy ever since. Well, them and all of us kids of course. There's six of us. Me and Port, and Eddy's kids. Penny is his youngest."

"I'm sorry. It sounds like she was important to you. I know the feeling." I leaned up against the gate next to her, feeling sorry that I'd brought it up.

"It's ok." A smile snuck into the corner of her mouth. "You'll have to ask Momma about her. If you get her started, she'll talk about Nori until you fall asleep. She tells the same old stories sometimes, but I always love hearing about her." She stopped and looked over to me. "You know the feeling, you said? I'm sorry."

I didn't want to move here and drop my drama on everyone. I came here to get away from all of that. I just wanted to start over. I figured Ruby was going to figure me out eventually, and it was okay to get to know each other as long as I made sure it stopped there.

"Yeah, that's... well. I'm pretty much on my own. It wasn't always like that, but it's just me these days."

"I'm sorry."

"Ahh it's alright. Looks like I'll have everything I need right here. At least for a while." Deflecting and trying to lighten the mood didn't really work. All it did was grab her attention. We ended up staring a bit too long again, long enough to make it awkward, and long enough that it meant something.

"So, your mom and the guys. Tell me more about this broad squad." Another attempt at deflecting. I spent enough time with the therapist. I saw my habits as they played out. I didn't mind talking, but I didn't really want to talk about myself. I was much more interested in anyone else, especially Ruby.

"Yeah, the broad squad. Dana, Ruth, Jane, and a few others. And of course, their respective husbands. They pretty much created this place. I mean, Wrightsville has always been here of course, growing slowly over the years. But the estate? That was all the broad squad. They got the gardens up and going, which paved the way for hosting events. Jane started the cafe, which turned into Cottage Row. Roger ended up growing the real estate side of that. Roger and Dana took this place from a beautiful home, to a business across the property.

"Roger used to joke with Port about running the place one day, but then it became less of a joke, and more of a plan. Dad and Eddy were ready to take over if Port wasn't, or if he just needed help. But Port and Penny were married and ready to take it on, so it all got handed over to them, legally anyway, a few years ago when Dana passed away. Then just last year they moved into the big house, and the kinks all got ironed out. Now that everyone's settled, well Port has some pretty big dreams for this place. Wrightsville is a growing tourist attraction, and Port wants to make sure that the estate grows with it. Between the property, the gardens, and the shrimp boat, the estate keeps a lot of people employed here in town... brings in a lot of tax dollars, too."

She finally took a breath and looked up to me. I had originally thought she couldn't possibly talk that much all the time. Maybe just when she met someone new. Sure enough, I think going a million miles a minute was a strength of hers, among others.

"Sorry. If you get me talking, I'll never stop. I bet you didn't care about most of that." She bit her lip, almost like she regretted telling me so much.

"Don't apologize." I said, "I'm enjoying learning about this place, and about your family." Then I caught up. "Wait, what shrimp boat?"

"Ahhhh..." she smiled. "The estate never ends. The Erv III, the shrimp boat you can usually see from the end of the pier, that's the Ervin's boat. Well, it's Port's now. But, Roger and Dana did that too."

"So, Port and Penny just inherited..."

"Pretty much the entire town," she laughed. "Crazy, huh? Roger and Dana had two kids of their own, but they moved to the city and never looked back. They visit now and then from Nashville, but they don't want the place. Neither one of them ever married or had any kids, so they were really supportive of handing it all down to Port, and of course they get a good share of the profits so they're also pretty supportive of anything Port wants to do to make improvements. It's perfect though. If anyone is a good fit to take over this place, it's my brother. The only thing he loves more than this property is Penny. We all knew they'd end up together, and it wasn't long before it became pretty clear that this place would become theirs too. All they've ever wanted, really."

"And what do you want?" I asked.

She breathed in through her teeth and shook her head. "Well, that's loaded."

"Sorry."

"No, it's okay. I don't really have any kind of plan. I just know I want to be here. The stables, the boys' photography sales, the cafe, surfing. I don't really have any intentions of giving all that up. It's working out so far, and I'm happy. What about you, where are you going?"

"Talk about loaded," I said.

"Hey, you started it."

"Well. I'm on my own. I don't really have anyone or anywhere to go home to. So I saw your brother's job posting online, that he was offering housing and the place was near the beach. I couldn't argue with any of that, so I emailed him my name and number, and here we are. So... where am I going? This afternoon I'm going to go find a new place for dinner. Where am I going in life? No telling. I'm not sure what I'm doing tomorrow."

"Tomorrow, you're cleaning stables. Next day, too. I'm going to need you to get busy if we're going to have these stables ready for new horses any time soon." It was clear she was trying to lighten the mood.

"Yes, ma'am." I said.

"Sorry, I didn't mean to be bossy." she laughed. "I'm really thankful for your help." The mood had shifted from chatty conversation while we kept busy, to some kind of deep get-to-know-you type of thing.

"Glad to do it."

She was blushing. It wasn't the first time, and I kind of enjoyed it.

She took a deep breath and stepped away from the fence, putting some distance between us. "I need to run to the cafe." She said, "I'm... I'll catch you later, then."

"Catch you later, Ruby." I watched her walk away, trying to think of other things. Like getting fired, becoming homeless, ruining a good opportunity. In my past life, maybe before I joined the Marines, Ruby would be a girl I'd set my sights on. Creative, hard working, funny, close with her family, and appreciative of a simple life. She had everything I wished I had, and hoped I'd find. But this wasn't the time or place to go falling for a girl like that. I hadn't gotten close to anyone other than the guys in my unit in years. I haven't so much as made a new friend since I got back to the states. And now I found myself feeling like I was part of a damned family, with my eyes glued to a beautiful girl, and my heart starting to crack open just a little bit. No one had been capable of doing that to me in years. But Ruby? She spills hot coffee on me and talks my ears off, and all of a sudden I was feeling alive again.

The balance between a working relationship and a safe distance from anyone getting hurt would be hard to find, but necessary. And not just for Ruby, but all of them. That's the only way I could stay here. If I got too close, someone would end up hurt. I'm the one who doesn't belong, and it would be me who would lose everything. I couldn't go through all of that again, I wouldn't make it.

Later that afternoon, after closing up the stables, and making a small repair to the barn roof, I made my way back toward the big house, running into Port when I got there. His truck pulling into the driveway was starting to feel less like a boss checking in, and more like a friend stopping by to say hello. He stepped out and held the door open as four little paws jumped down to the ground next to him. He looked back into the truck, and whistled. Another set of paws quickly followed.

"Hey, Hobie. How was your morning?" He asked.

"Good. Was just about to check in, actually, and see what you needed for the rest of this afternoon." Realizing we were suddenly up a dog from the last time I checked, I continued, "So, two dogs. What did I miss?" I knelt down to play with Maggie, and the second dog who looked just like her.

"Yeah... I haven't exactly asked Penny yet, so if you see her maybe just keep this to yourself for a bit. But, this little guy was in Maggie's litter, and turns out he isn't doing so well cooped up in an apartment. The owners brought him back to the family the puppies all came from, and then I got a phone call. They know I have a weakness... and I think now we have two dogs." Port looked excited, but also concerned about what kind of trouble he'd gotten himself into. "Penny will love him, I'm sure. But I'm still gonna get in trouble." He laughed. "His name is Bark."

"I'm sorry." I stammered and laughed. "The dog's name is Bark? Like b-a-r-k? *Bark?*"

"Yep. Apparently that's what happens when you let a four year old name a dog. Damn thing answers to it, follows commands and everything. There's no changing his name now. So..." He stretched his hand out toward the puppies. "Maggie and.... Bark." He smiled, and bent to scratch their ears. He wasn't kidding about having a weakness; it was obvious. And I knew exactly why they called him about a homeless puppy.

"Alrighty then." Bark. That was going to give me something to laugh at for quite some time. "Well hey, I've finished up with the stables, and that leak was an easier fix than we thought. So, what else can I do for you, boss?"

"Ruby seems to think you're pretty quick with the horses. It sounds like maybe you should take a break, Hobie. And, it is Sunday you know. So, there's that whole weekend idea; we're pretty fond of weekends."

"That's okay, I just want to get as much done for you as I can. Seems like you have some big goals for this place."

"Sounds like you're used to keeping busy."

"Sure. I guess Marines aren't exactly known for slacking on the job." The tension in my shoulders built instantly, like my muscles were preparing to have my gear on again. The vest, the boots—it was all a well known outfit, and just the thought of it jumped me back into go-mode. I didn't know how to work a job like this, not having every minute of every day accounted for, and always having more to do. I didn't know how to fit in here. As much as I enjoyed this place, it still didn't feel like a spot here was carved out for me. That's the way people talk about families and small towns. That's the way Marines would talk about going home, or feeling like they couldn't. Everyone just wants to be where they belong. I still wasn't sure if such a place existed for me.

"Tell you what, Hobie. Our deal is good. The house is yours, and the work is, well... it's pretty fluid. We're not always going to have ten hours of work a day. And believe it or not, we expect you to take days off now and then, and relax, have some fun. I'm sure you're going to be more help than we could have imagined. But maybe, go enjoy yourself? Make some friends? Go fishing? Learn to surf? I don't want you getting burned out. I want you to enjoy being here, too."

"Fair enough." I said, "Can't hurt I guess, learning how to relax. You think of anything though, you just let me know. Whatever you need."

"I appreciate that." Port thought for a second, and continued. "For now, I'm plenty happy with what you're doing. As long as Ruby is happy with your work at the stables, and Penny is happy with your work in the gardens—"

I interrupted him there. "Actually it sounds like all she needs right now is help with watering everything and picking weeds here and there. That's taken care of, no worries. Actually when you get a chance I wanted to talk to you about building an irrigation system. But, no rush on that. I can take care of things the old fashioned way for the time being."

"Well, now look at that. New ideas are just as helpful as hands on work. Soon here I'll be teaching you a bit more about how you can help the guys on the Erv, and then I'll probably have you learn a few things to help me out with the marina. But... let's do that slowly. I don't want you quitting on me."

"No, sir." I laughed. "Wouldn't dream of it."

"Alrighty, well. Go have fun or something. There's a ton of boards and stuff in the garage, and there's a spare key to one of the old boats hanging on the hook in the mudroom. Yours whenever you want."

I stood up and shook his hand. "Thanks, man. For everything. Call when you need me?"

"Absolutely." Port added, standing and walking inside. "See you later." He patted his hand on his thigh a few times, and the dogs followed behind him. They were wobbly and stumbling in all the ways you'd expect for dogs with paws five sizes too big. They were going to make great family dogs, especially for the boys. I was a bit excited, too, to see how Penny reacted to the accidental addition to the family.

The only explanation to my setup here was luck, or maybe a divine mistake—landing a job, and a home, with people like this. But I wasn't about to lose it, that's for sure. I finally found myself some place that felt safe. A place that didn't have loss hanging over it. A place where I wasn't feeling my mom or my brother being gone. I'd finally found myself in a place where I could just keep busy, work hard, rest well, and get through my day. For the first time in a long time, I could go to sleep at night and not wonder if I'd wake up in the morning. I didn't fear what might come the next day. Here, I could put everything down.

Maybe I was doing a bit better than I gave myself credit for. I didn't particularly feel like I was family, but then again it hadn't been too long. Maybe the idea that this was a safe *place* was enough for now.

Overseas, we'd refer to this as a neutralized threat. I'd been desperate to feel this way, and it sure took long enough. Ruby was a nice part of all of that. And the puppies didn't hurt. *Bark*. I laughed again as I walked away. What a stupid name for a dog.

THE ESTATE

SIX

Hobie

Three in the morning comes quickly, that's for sure. I was used to working at all hours of the day or night, but it had been a while since I was up and working in what I considered to be the middle of the night. Port wanted me to spend a day on the shrimp boat with the guys so that I'd be able to help them out from time to time. So, later that week we made a plan. And that plan started with meeting in the kitchen at three thirty.

"I don't really need you to know how to work on the boat as much as I need you to understand how to get to them, get back home, and how to communicate with them and the Coast Guard over the radio." He stood in front of the refrigerator like he was hoping breakfast would just magically appear. "It would be extremely helpful if you at least got familiar with any of the equipment or tools they may need from us at the marina. I want

81

you to take some time to get to know the guys on the boat too, because whatever comes up or whatever they may need, you're going to be their man." He started packing up a cooler on the kitchen island when Ruby walked through the door.

"Morning, fellas!" Ruby smacked me on the back as she passed me, heading over to start brewing a fresh pot of coffee.

"You're... awake." I said. Just then, Penny rounded the bottom of the staircase. The girls both moved around the kitchen like they'd already had a pot or two of coffee themselves. The process was obviously familiar to them, pouring cereal and tossing waffles into the toaster oven like they were used to running an assembly line.

"Big day?" Port asked, reaching into the pantry.

"Not really, just that early catering for the university I was telling you about," Penny said.

Ruby elaborated. "The chancellor pissed off the county commissioners and now they're having us bring a big old breakfast over to campus so they can make everyone shake hands and smile for the camera." She reached for the creamer in the fridge and slid the bottle across the island. They just kept moving like factory workers. No one missed a beat.

"Do you always have early morning events?" I asked. Standing still, trying to stay out of the way.

"Absolutely not." Ruby blurted out, waving a finger in the air. "I don't mind mornings. But *this* is night time, there's not even a hint of sunlight. I don't like this."

"Yet, here you are." Port said. There was that sibling banter I was enjoying so much.

"Yeah well, you know what it's like to get *voluntold* to handle things at the cafe. Mom wasn't exactly asking. Tips can't be too bad, though. They'll probably compete to see who has the bigger wallet, and I don't hate when they do that." Ruby pressed the lid into her coffee mug and slapped her hands on the counter. "Alright, early birds. Let's get this show on the road."

"Oh, Port." A devious smile crossed Penny's face. "Speaking of *voluntold*. Since you came home with a new dog, I thought maybe you wouldn't mind being responsible for... all of that. So, if you could feed them, and walk them, and well... all of that."

Port rolled his eyes.

"What was I supposed to do? Let Bark go to a shelter?" He gave her puppy dog eyes. Real, legitimate, puppy dog eyes about a puppy, which was pretty entertaining.

"He's right. If you'd heard about that dog at the shelter you would have brought him home anyway." Ruby sipped her coffee again, choking on it as she laughed. "Bark. That's the dumbest thing I've ever heard. Good thing they're so cute." She reached down and scratched their heads on the way out the door.

I didn't want to find her so funny, or so entertaining. I didn't want to find myself hung up on every word she said. I wished she owned a slightly less flattering pair of jeans. But this just wasn't going away. Keeping my eyes off Ruby was getting more difficult each day. I had to remind myself over and over to ignore it, and to ignore her. Keeping my distance was for her own good, but it wasn't doing me a damn bit of good. I needed to get out of this kitchen fast.

"Port, I'll meet you down at the marina." I didn't wait for an answer before I stepped out the door and jumped off the porch, making my way down the hill to the dock. I cursed myself every step of the way. I had no business spending time with Ruby. I had no business falling into this family at all. In the end, they would only end up hurt, just like everyone else I've ever loved. This had to be strictly business. Business, and a place to live. It had to end there.

They all must have followed me out. "Have a good day!" I heard Ruby holler behind me. I tossed up a wave without turning back. I couldn't.

I reached the boat and crashed onto the bench. I started the box breathing exercises I'd learned when we all got shipped home from deployment. In through the nose and out through the mouth was supposed to help calm a racing heart. I sat there for a few minutes, trying my best to let it go, to remind myself that if I stayed away, they'd all be fine. I couldn't stand the idea of hurting them. Especially the boys. Between the Dixons and everyone else in town, this family had it all, and I worried that I was going to ruin that. I worried that I would ruin *them*.

"You took off pretty quick back there... you alright?" Port stepped up onto the boat with his cooler, handing me a coffee mug. "You ran out before the coffee was done. Penny said you like yours black. So, here you go."

"Sorry about that. Got distracted thinking through a few things, that's all." I stepped back away from the helm, but Port sat down, running his hand over his face like he was choosing his words carefully.

"You know, I've been thinking. You're about the hardest worker I've ever met, and I've only known you for a few weeks now." Port leaned back, sipping his coffee, and threw an ankle over his knee, settling into his seat before he continued. "You don't take breaks. You don't stop for fun. You never leave to visit anyone, and to the best of my knowledge, no one has been here to visit you."

"That's all true." I replied.

"Well, are you doing okay? Anything I can do for you?"

Port didn't seem as if he was accusing me of anything. Instead it seemed as if he... worried. As if this family had any room to be any more perfect, my boss was worried about me. I had a boss who cared enough about me to notice my lack of... a life, and think about it long enough to wonder why.

"I just like to stick to myself, sir. I don't exactly have experience in a place like this. With a big family, close friends, and all. Kind of figure it's just best for me to stick to what I know." I sat down across from him on the bench seats. "Seems like y'all are glued at the elbows around here. Just not sure I fit in, or that I would even know how."

"Hobie..." Port sipped his coffee. "This is a really small town. Honestly, it really is more like a large family than a small town. But, we don't take it lightly when someone new moves in.

Remember, I hired you. I wouldn't have asked you to move here if I didn't think you'd get along with my family, with everyone here on the estate. So, if that's what you're worried about, I can at least tell you that Penny and I, and the boys, we're glad you're here. Ruby too, and our parents. Everyone's really glad you're here."

"Me too, sir."

"Just Port, bud. Just Port." He raised his coffee mug to me with a nod.

"Port. Right. I really appreciate everything. I think maybe I just need to adjust. Going from my old world, to this here, well... it's a big change. Everyone here is happy. So calm, and polite. The routine here is new for me. Sorry if I've been too closed off. I'll try to get to know y'all better, really."

I didn't want to say too much more than that. I knew I had to acknowledge the fact that I was quiet and distant. But I didn't want to overload them with the weight I carried with me. The loss, losing everyone I've ever cared about. I didn't need to bring them down with all of that. But I also didn't think I was going to get off that easy; Port didn't miss a beat.

"You're getting to know us plenty, man. It's you. We'd really like the opportunity to get to know *you* better. When you're ready. Until then..." He slapped his knees and stood up. "Why don't we go catch us some shrimp." He tossed me the keys to the boat.

"Alright. First things first, I want you to know how to find them, and how to get to them." Port spent about twenty minutes going over the navigation system, their radio, and the boat itself. Not completely self explanatory, but easy enough to learn.

The ride out to the Erv seemed like a standard morning commute. Port knew each boat and where they were heading. After passing each one with a simple wave, we pulled up to the Erv and Port tied us to the side of it and led the way up onto the deck.

It was another group that had obviously done this a time or two before, like the girls with breakfast. They moved around that boat like they were raised there, and knew every nook and cranny of the place. We stood out of the way as he explained to me who each person was and what they were doing. The sun was just coming up over the horizon, and the guys here were already well into a busy day of work.

"I just want you to see it all. You'll get to know these guys over time. They're always at dinner telling their stories, making me a bit more afraid every day about leaving them all out here alone." He laughed with his hands on his hips. "These kids are wild, but Hugo takes good care of them. No one's died yet... at least that I'm aware of."

I knew he was being sarcastic, but the comment sparked a bit of anxiety in me. The thought of being on this boat when something awful happened made me sick to my stomach. I figured I would just try to minimize my time out here. The more time I could spend working on my own, the less chance I'd have of being tied to anything that went wrong.

A husky, older gentleman, stepped through a sliding glass door and onto the deck. He had a thick white beard, and was wearing a bucket hat that looked like it had seen a few more years than it was intended to. He had bright yellow waders on, with suspenders over a plaid shirt that looked just as old as the hat. His boots sloshed with each step as he walked across the deck and over to us, handing us each a paper cup full of fried shrimp.

"Morning, Hugo!" Port said, tossing the first shrimp up into the air and moving around to catch the bite in his mouth.

When he caught it, a bunch of the guys cheered. "You're up to seventeen days, man!"

"Seventeen days?" I asked.

Port thunked on his chest like Tarzan and then took a dramatic bow. "Seventeen days since I last dropped a shrimp, thank you very much. Care to take a bet?"

"Oh no, I'll eat mine the old fashioned way." I laughed. "I don't stand a chance beating you at that."

Hugo reached out to shake my hand. "Young man, I'm Houghton Gillmore. Everyone calls me Hugo. My grandson is friends with Port's boys so I'm sure you'll see him around. It's nice to meet you. I hear you're living in Ruby's old place?"

A few of the guys dropped what they were doing and walked over to join in the conversation.

"Really?"

"Ruby's place?"

"Have you met her yet?" I heard.

I looked at Port, overwhelmed with why my living arrangements were of such concern, but reached out to continue shaking hands through the group.

"Uh, yes. I'm Hobie. I just moved into the guest house... Ruby's place. Yes. And uh, yeah I've been working the stables with her a bit now. Are y'all friends of hers?" It occurred to me then that they were all about the same age and I was in the self proclaimed 'smallest fishing town in North Carolina'. So *are y'all friends* was probably a stupid question, and was quickly validated when a few of the guys laughed.

"Well, Ruby and our wives all grew up together, graduated together, went to Carolina together, and now everyone's back." One of the guys, who looked an awful lot like Hugo, said. "I'm Junior," he continued. "And this is Blue, Stitch, Hoke, and Stewart."

I couldn't help laughing out loud, seeing as how that last one didn't quite fit the list. "Stewart?" I asked.

Stewart rolled his eyes and explained as the rest of the boys laughed. "Junior is actually a junior. Blue over there got his nickname because he almost drowned on his first day. Stitch, because he's only worked here six months and has managed to get stitches nineteen times. Hoke over there went to Virginia Tech and tells us that a Hokie is some sort of bird. And I'm Stewart. I'm the big city boy who gets made fun of almost daily for trying to *go country*. The fellas here just can't stand the thought of someone enjoying hard and dirty work, but still appreciating the city life and dressing nice."

Junior chimed back in. "He also sounds like the most Northern Yankee ever to grace the land of the pines. But we love him anyway."

Port stepped in then. "Alright, alright. Look. I want Hobie to spend some time out here today to see what y'all do. If you need anything, he'll probably be your runner. So teach him well. And for the love of God try not to let him get hurt?" He shot his eyes right over to Stitch.

"No problem, boss man. I'll take good care of him. Scout's honor."

"Oh, I feel much better." Port joked. "Hugo, please?"

"No problem, son." Hugo answered, continuing on his cup full of shrimp.

The guys all scattered and Port checked in with me before taking off. "Is that alright with you, Hobie? I figured that Hugo and the guys can teach you better than I can. I have to hit the road with Sam. He's got a soccer game this afternoon. Hugo can bring you back to the marina in a few hours, in time for whatever lunch the girls bring back?"

"Absolutely." I said.

The morning on the boat went pretty smoothly. I just did my best to stay out of the way and watch. Teamwork was a common theme around here, both at home and out here on the boat. The crew worked together through the process so easily. I started to wonder if this kind of ease was something that came with being born and raised in a small town. Maybe they were so used to each other, that it couldn't possibly go any other way.

They almost reminded me a bit of my old unit. We knew each other so well that I could describe the way my sargeant blinked. I knew how many minutes it would take to wake up my guys in time for chow. I knew that Darryl had to put his left shoe on first, because his right foot was unlucky. I knew their favorite songs, their wildest stories. We all knew what the other was going to do before they did it. We had a strong team. That is, until I lost them all.

The guys on the Erv seemed a lot like that. The way they knew each other showed in their work. And wouldn't you know it, Stitch made it a whole four hours without a single injury. He only tripped and fell, jamming a few fingers. No stitches required, which I figured Port would be glad to hear.

By the time I got back to the marina shortly after lunch time, I had absorbed a lot more knowledge about shrimping, and about Ruby. I wasn't prepared for the social chatter on the boat. As it turned out, they were serious when they said that all of their wives were friends with Ruby. Best friends, apparently.

I hadn't met them yet, but it sounded like I'd probably looked right past them. To the best of my understanding, Lottie was usually in the water with Ruby in the mornings. Jackie-Ann stopped by the cafe every day to get croissants and coffee for her office staff. Blake owned a boutique on Topsail. And Birdie, though I wasn't certain I heard that name right, could usually be found at home with her own four children, as well as Jackie-Ann's little one. I hadn't seen Ruby with her friends yet, but I also think I hadn't been looking. It sounded nice, the life Ruby shared with her friends. I wanted to know it, to be a part of it.

And with that, it seemed like the guys all took a personal interest in my working with her at the stables and moving into her old house. I only had to clarify four times that Ruby had in fact moved out, and that I was indeed living there alone. And not *with* Ruby.

They questioned me like older brothers.

Did I find her attractive? Of course I did.

Had I seen her surf? No, but now that you mention it...

How's everything going with the family? Fine. Why did that matter? I'm here to work.

It was clear that they all had their ideas; ideas that I certainly didn't want to fight. But I knew better; I couldn't have her. I could never have her. I didn't even deserve the chance.

And of course, after playing twenty questions all about Ruby, I was back at the cottage thinking of the only thing I shouldn't be thinking about. Time to get to work.

On the way back out of the house, toolbox in hand and headed to fix a few shingles on the barn roof, I found a note taped to the porch.

"Hobie. I really do think you're in the right place. Let some people get to know you. Not much going on around town tonight, so we're having an extra dinner tonight over at the house. Everyone will be there. Why don't you give it a shot. - Port."

If only it was that easy. If I could just be that guy that strikes up a conversation and a friendship with anyone that walks by. Wouldn't that be something, if I wasn't the guy that ruined everyone around him.

SEVEN

Ruby

"You missed, that's E! H-O-R-S-E! I won!" I heard Roy yelling to Sam as I got out of the Jeep and walked toward the house.

"Did not!" Sam countered. "MeMaw said I could have a practice shot. Right MeMaw?"

My mom tossed her hands in the air, waving herself out of the conversation. "Nope. I ain't getting in between that one, boys. I don't know a darn thing about that game. Just play. And would you just be nice! For just a minute!"

"Hey, toss it here!" I broke in. Roy was pretty stellar on a surfboard, and Sam was already getting eyed for travel soccer teams for high school. But when it came to basketball, those boys were useless. It made for a good time at dinner though. Right on time, the old guys walked up to the driveway hooting and hollering about whooping up on the youngins'. I dribbled a bit and took a shot, which I missed as usual, and then I walked over to the lawn chairs and joined the ladies to watch this week's edition of the men versus the boys, which always turned into the grown ups looking like fools. And I always enjoyed it.

Mom handed me a drink before plopping into the chair next to me, and then the order had fallen back into place. Penny, myself, Mom, Grammy Ruth, Allison, and even Nori's mom who was in town for a visit. We sat and watched as the boys all picked up a game of basketball, with a typical wager between the adults: winner gets a beer. Things were just picking up when I heard Hugo in the driveway. You didn't even have to see him to know who it was, since he had wired his horn to play the Dukes of Hazzard dixie song. Obnoxious, but hilarious. When he slowed down enough to park, the boys and their wives all jumped out of the bed of the truck and came our way.

"The Erv crew has arrived!" Hugo shouted. "The par-tay can officially start. Who has my beer?"

Dad tossed Hugo a can, and the girls all opened up their chairs and settled on the sidelines with us. I enjoyed this time with them, when their babies were home with a sitter, their husbands were occupied, and I didn't feel like the odd one out. Dinner was one of those times where I really just got to be one of the girls again, like they hadn't all grown up and started a family while I sat around by myself.

"This is one of my favorite things, sitting here with you girls." Grammy Ruth started. Her voice was slow and shaky these days, but beautiful to hear, even if it was the same few comments she made each week. "It hasn't gotten old, you know. This group dinner thing started all the way back when Roger, Dana, Jane and I were just kids ourselves. Here we are, two..." she shook her hands at the boys like she was confused. "two and a half, I guess, generations later. And it's all just the same."

"I hope you're happy with this town you've raised." Aunt Allison answered.

"Can you imagine what things would be like? If Roger and Dana hadn't grown this place to what it is? Can you imagine if Jane never started the cafe?" Penny wondered out loud. "Where do you think we'd be?"

"We wouldn't be." I said. "You and me, anyway. Jane and the cafe... she's the only reason your parents got together. And if that hadn't happened, well we all know Mom and Dad never would have figured their own mess out."

"That's the truth." Mom laughed. "Rhett wouldn't have known what being an adult was like if Eddy and Nori hadn't done it first. And we certainly wouldn't be together if it wasn't for the two of them getting married." She laughed as she wiped a tear from her eye. I knew that it made her sad, thinking of Aunt Nori. They were best friends. But I also know how happy it made her, sitting here, watching the life they made together play out.

"That wedding." Allison added. "That was the biggest beer fest I've ever been to, to this day."

"And yet you were sober enough that you still remember everything that happened," Mom answered with a sarcastic grin.

"Oh please. We'd all been waiting on you and Rhett forever. You two idiots kept running away from a good thing and we were all sick of it. It's because of the two of you making out on the dance floor that we all got so drunk anyway. Y'all gave us even more to celebrate."

"Good lord." I said. "Y'all are supposed to be old and boring. Not talking about making out and drinking at parties."

"You think we didn't have fun when we were your age?" Aunt Allison leaned forward in her chair.

"Ha. Trust me." Mom took a sip. "We learned from the best. Dana, Mom, and Jane — they kept this town on their toes. So Allison, Nori, and I just carried on the family tradition. We made sure we got plenty of experience before teaching the six of y'all how to try growing up here." Everyone laughed.

"Oh believe me. All of your *experience* is well known around here. I'll never get away from being Rhett and Amy's sweet surprise." I stuck my tongue out to mom. It was a well known fact that I, born an unplanned and long number of years after Port, was the tiny little light that blew this town back up.

"What can I say?" mom continued. "You're the grown up now. Your turn to take this place on, and make it your own."

"We'll see. I have no intentions of creating the next generation all by myself, but thank you for the confidence." I sighed. I wasn't interested in a single man on this island. I grew up with all of them and they were either married, gay, or more trouble than they were worth.

"Seems to me, Port may have solved that problem." Mom added lightly. The ladies all laughed under their breath.

"Alright, alright. That's enough." Jackie-Ann had tried a number of times to set me up with guys she knew from college, which obviously never worked out. Since then, I did my best to avoid being shuffled into some girlfriend-concocted-relationship. I took the opportunity to see myself out of that conversation, and went inside to change.

I peeked from the upstairs window as the game ended and everyone came inside to start getting dinner ready. I came back downstairs and into the kitchen with a towel draped over my shoulders. I promised the boys I'd swim with them at dinner. When I didn't swim with them the week before, they accused me of being an old lady who was just waiting for her time to join the broad squad. If that wasn't a slap across the face, I don't know what would be. So tonight, they sure as heck wouldn't find me hanging with the ladies. Nope, I was going to dive into that pool with those boys and show them who's boss. Who's a young boss, I mean.

Mom and Aunt Allison were sitting at the island, eating some of Uncle Eddy's pasta salad, both dropping forks, whispering, and looking over to each other when I walked in.

"Well spill it, then." I said. "No use being all awkward and trying to hide whatever it is the two of y'all were just talking about." I laid my towel on the countertop and started to fix myself a bowl. I never missed an opportunity for that pasta salad.

"Come on then, let's have it. Don't be ridiculous." I sat down and took a bite.

"Well," mom started, "Allison was just telling me she's got a whole bunch of free time this week, and offered to spend it with me in the cafe. So, we were just thinking that might give you some extra time to help out around here, maybe show Hobie a bit more of the town."

"Okay, y'all couldn't be subtle if you tried." I rolled my eyes and took a bite, "God, that's good."

"Oh, honey." My Aunt Allison always played good cop. She knew I couldn't get upset with her. "We're not trying to get in your business. We just think he's a mighty sweet man. Port seems to like him. And the boys sure are enjoying having him around. He's polite, he's—"

"Oh for the love of God, out with it, Allison." Mom cut her off, pointing her fork at me. "That man is drop dead gorgeous and he can't keep his eyes off of you."

"Mom!" I dropped my face to my hands. I knew I wouldn't be able to hide the blush. "So what if he's handsome. Port hired him to help out with the property, not date his sister. Just let the man do his job."

"Oh honey, Port knew darn well that you'd find that boy attractive. He may be of the male species but Port's not a complete idiot." Mom was blunt when it came to sharing her opinions. She didn't care who was listening. And it seemed that worked out just the way she intended.

Port stuck his head through the kitchen door, knocking on the wall to announce his presence.

"Now, I don't mean to interrupt," he began. "Well, yes I do."

"Oh come on, Port." I groaned, standing to take my bowl to the sink. I'd hoped that getting up and walking away would help end the conversation.

"No, now you wait a minute. Just hear me out. He applied for the job all on his own, it's not like I went looking for him. I gave him the interview because he's got a college degree and he's fresh out of the military. So I figured I'd at least have a hard worker who was able to learn. And what we ended up with was a hard worker, a fast learner, who also happens to be one of the most polite, selfless, and generous guys any of us have ever met. So excuse me for not being bothered when I noticed he's also got eyes for my beautiful baby sister, who I love so much." At least his added drama was something to laugh about.

"Alright, alright now you're just making fun." I leaned back on the counter, arms crossed against my chest.

"I'm your brother. It's my job." He leaned forward and kissed my forehead. "Now, that's all I'm going to say about that. Except of course maybe it would be reasonable for me to let you know that I *did* invite him to dinner tonight, and he declined. I think. So if you wanted to head on over there and try yourself, maybe you'd have a better shot at it."

"Y'all are not going to let up on this, are you?" I asked.

"Nope." They all replied in unison, sharing that same smug grin.

"Ugh," I groaned. "I'm going swimming. I promised Sam and Roy I wouldn't be all adult and boring tonight. I'm pretty sure this qualifies. So, goodbye." I grabbed my towel and walked out of the kitchen, across the porch and down to the pool. I heard Mom and Aunt Allison laughing through the screen door.

"What took you so long?" Roy yelled as I walked up to the pool.

"Nothing. Your dad's just giving me a hard time. And your MeMaw wanted to talk about the cafe. Sorry, boys. I'm here now." I tossed a football to Sam and dove in after it.

When I came back up above the surface, I barely had two whole seconds to wipe my eyes before I had four arms and legs wrapped around me, trying to take me under. Keeping ten year old boys entertained was exhausting. I loved getting to be involved in their lives everyday, though. The forced workouts didn't hurt either.

The truth is, I really admired the family Port had made for himself, and I hoped that one day I'd find something similar. A family of my own always sounded like a good plan, but growing up here allowed me to eliminate most of the local boys from my future plans. I learned over the years that it was rare for a man to come to a town like this with intentions of staying. Wrightsville was charming, but it was small, and you could fairly assume that there would never be many career opportunities here for outsiders to come in for.

After about thirty minutes of trying my hardest not to drown at the hands of Sam and Roy, Dad hollered from the porch that dinner was ready. We all jumped out of the pool, and I dried off, and tossed a tank top on over my suit before heading back up to the porch to eat. The boys didn't bother to dry off, after Dad mentioned shrimp kabobs. Smart, really. The kabobs wouldn't last more than five minutes.

I took my plate to the table and joined the ladies and a few of Ruth's friends from bingo night in town. Before I knew it I was hearing the familiar beginnings of the year that Eddy met Nori, the year the town's most popular love story began.

It was almost like Eddy and Nori were a romance novel never written. Instead, their story lived in the minds of the women in town. The women and Uncle Eddy, of course. He was still one of the most eligible bachelors anyone around here knew of, but he was getting older, and there weren't many available women in town his age. It didn't matter though. Uncle Eddy always swore that Nori was his one and only—he had his great love and was just waiting until the day he got to be with her again. He had no interest in finding another, certain that the most perfect love was just waiting for him on the other side.

It was an easy story to listen to. Mom and Dad were known for defying the odds and coming out on top, but Eddy and Nori were known for easy love. The kind of relationship where everything is right from the very beginning, and nothing ever got in the way. Mom even swears they never fought. Dad said that wasn't true. Apparently he brought Uncle Eddy home drunk one night and Aunt Nori made it pretty clear that she wore the pants in that house. But no one else had heard it, and no one else was willing to say they believed it.

Aunt Nori was always the girl for him. He'd had plenty of fun in his younger years, but no one really talked about that Eddy anymore, almost as if he didn't even exist. The day Nori came to town and almost drowned, that was the day that the Eddy we all know and love came into existence—the Eddy that belonged to Nori.

I dreamed of that kind of story and that kind of family. I wanted a family like the one I was raised in, one that started with incredible relationships built from the ground up. You could say I was a dreamer or a bit of a romantic, but I'd never spent any time dating around, even in college. I wasn't interested in dating just anyone. I wanted to find the right guy for me. I wanted to find the one, and fall completely in love, to the point of no return. I didn't want to do what my mom had warned me about, doing the friends with benefits thing. She said it only ever ended in a broken heart.

In fact, no one ever talked about it much, but Eddy ditched my mom just in time to make himself available for Nori. It's kind of weird, knowing that my mom and Uncle Eddy used to be... together... not really dating just... well, I tried not to think about that. But, as fate would have it, that was right about the time that Dad fell into mom's life too. And the closer Eddy and Nori got, the more opportunities mom and dad had to cross paths. And, well, the rest is history. The happily ever after kind.

A few minutes went by while I listened to everyone talk about the good old days and young love. It didn't take too long for the conversation to go full circle and get brought back around to me.

"Now Eddy and Nori, that was some love. One for the ages, you might say." Grammy Ruth was slower with words these days, but she was quick with wit and enjoyed stirring the pot. "Wouldn't it be something if a love like that found its way to you." She looked at me with wide eyes as she took a bite from her kabob.

"Oh give it a rest, Grammy. He's handsome. I get it." I said, "Can we please just—"

"Oh please. You've had your chance with every boy in college and every tourist since then that wandered over that bridge after you, and you would never give any of them the time of day. We all know you're looking for a man who wants to stay right here and be Mr. Wrightsville. And wouldn't you know it, your brother just brought in a damn good candidate."

"Language, Ruth." Penny chimed in from a few seats down, pointing to the boys. "Little ears, ladies. And repetitive mouths." She looked back at me. "She's right though, Port mentioned a while back that he wouldn't be surprised if you found yourself interested in the new hire."

"Wait a second. Have you all been planning this behind my back? This whole time?" I laughed, frustrated, not sure how I should feel about everyone ganging up on me like this.

"We're not conspiring, dear." Ruth's voice shook.

"Of course not," mom added. "But we sure aren't going to sit here and pretend like we don't see the possibilities either."

"See what?" I asked. "He's just here to work. He's obviously not interested. He isn't even here at dinner."

"I tried!" Port yelled across the table. This was getting out of control.

"Oh for the love of—" I stood up from the table with my dishes. "I'm leaving. I've got to get up early in the morning." I started to walk away, but Aunt Allison took one last shot.

"Yes, sweetheart. Hobie's probably looking forward to another morning at the stables with you. Make sure you put on those cute jeans tomorrow! Those darker ones from J. Crew." I walked into the house, but she only got louder. "THEY MAKE YOUR BEHIND LOOK—"

I dropped my dishes in the sink loud enough that they could all hear the clatter on the porch. Laughter continued and I grabbed my phone from the bowl on the counter and headed back out to the Jeep. Uncle Eddy caught me off guard on the front porch.

"Hey." I groaned.

"Oh sugar. They love you." He looked comfy as could be in that rocking chair, staring out into the gardens.

"Well sometimes their love is a little agressive."

"Well, sweetie." He patted his hand on the chair next to him. "I know that no amount of pestering from the town can change what is or isn't supposed to happen."

"Jane bugged in on you and Aunt Nori, though." I countered. "And they're doing the same thing to me."

"Yes, she did." His smile couldn't be contained. "But Nori was made for me, whether the old ladies interfered or not." He adjusted his hat, and sniffled a bit, which I knew was his attempt at holding back a few tears. "Point is, they're doing it because they love you. And life is short. So I figure we're all better off, if we just let them love in whatever way they know how. No matter how much it may interfere with your love life."

"Hobie is not here for my love life." I argued.

"We'll see," he answered, and stood as I rolled my eyes. "You know I can't help it. I'm a hopeless romantic." He winked, and kissed me on the cheek.

"You better get back there before you miss out on all the good stuff." I stepped off the porch and turned back to find him holding his empty plate, and his beer. "Nevermind," I laughed. "I love you."

"I love you too, sugar. Don't miss the good stuff, okay?"

He walked inside and I climbed into the Jeep, thinking about what he said. I think he was a sentimental man before he found Nori. But losing her only highlighted that side of him. He always had something to say that reminded you of the importance of love, and of friendships. Not much else mattered, and he always found a way to remind us that life was short. *Don't miss the good stuff.*

THE ESTATE

I cranked the radio up as loud as I could, hoping to interrupt any conversation about me that might still be lingering, and I drove home.

EIGHT

Ruby

The chimes of a new text message weren't usually enough to wake me up, but the repeated chimes of the boys texting me at six in the morning would do it. Over and over again, that light beep sounded until it felt more like a death alarm. I caved, and rolled over to check my phone, and make sure someone wasn't dead.

Better be good. I thought, as I opened my messages. Seventeen missed text messages from the boys, about covering for them if their mom found out they skipped school again to surf. *Sorry, boys.*

I laughed as I read the messages that followed from Penny.

I know you didn't tell them they could skip school.
And don't you dare cover for them.

They're grounded, and on dish duty for a month. And weekend stables duty until you say otherwise, for lying and trying to blame you for it.

That reminds me. Come over tonight around five for dinner. I'll be in the gardens this afternoon too, if you've got time.

I enjoyed starting my days in the stables. I enjoyed the time even more when Hobie was there to share the workload I never even asked, he just showed up every day, ready to work. The good view helped the time fly by too. But I certainly wouldn't complain about sleeping in now and then while the boys took care of the barn. A few people usually found benefit in the boys getting in trouble, and I was usually one of them. With an estate full of chores, getting grounded around here usually came with a list of hard labor. Dad and Uncle Eddy always had us scrub boats. Port and Penny are fans of punishment on land, since the twins love the water so much. It didn't take too long to realize that they enjoyed getting punished by boat labor. It just gave them another reason to be out under the sun.

I was pleasantly surprised when I got to the stables to find Hobie already with the horses. I kept myself hidden behind the barn door, and listened while he talked to them.

"You two sure are spoiled, living here. Especially with Ruby. She's a beauty, huh Tigua?" I giggled as Tigua answered with a sigh, and Hobie continued like they were having a two-sided conversation.

"I know. She's pretty funny too, huh? Ask her about the coffee next time you see her. That's a good one." He stood and rubbed down Tigua's side, circling to his other side, and getting started with the next hoof. "And tell her that was my good shirt." I tried my best to muffle my laugh. But I was smiling wider than I had in a long time.

"I don't know, buddy." Hobie continued. "I just don't want to get too close, you know?" Tigua sighed again, and I felt a sense of relief as I picked up on the friendship that had grown between a lonely man and an old horse.

"You're an old man." Hobie said. "Any advice? Any ideas?" He laughed to himself as he finished up with Tigua's hooves and stood again, taking the reins and leading Tigua out to the field. I followed far enough behind that I could just admire the two of them, and the way they were together. Hobie climbed up onto the fence and watched as Tigua joined Sampson out on the edge of the property by the water.

I made my way over to the fenceline, and leaned in next to Hobie.

"Making friends, huh?" I climbed up to join him as he answered.

"Hey. Uh, yeah, I guess so."

"Good choice. They won't tell your secrets." He just smiled at me. "What's in store for you today?"

"I'm meeting Penny in the gardens after lunch. We're going to go ahead and draw out some possible designs for a new irrigation system. I think we're going to install some barrels to collect rainwater, and start trying to use that for the property while we're at it."

"That's a wonderful idea. You can do all that?" I was impressed, with both his attention to earth friendly ideas, as well as his plans to help the estate grow over the long term.

"Might take some learning, but it's nothing I can't figure out. More work upfront, but more payoff over time."

"That's neat. I'm excited to see what you come up with." We turned back out to watch the horses, and the tide. "I think you're exactly what we needed around here. Tell me you know how to renovate houses and I'll think the good Lord sent you here himself." I joked.

"Actually, I learned a lot overseas, and might be able to help. What did you have in mind?"

"Oh, you name it, it probably needs to be done. Uncle Eddy is working on a list. I've got big ideas for the house." It brought me so much joy, being back in my childhood home. While I wanted to give it a touch of my own design, I also wanted to make sure the house would stand long enough for my children, and their children, to grow up there and appreciate it the way I still do. In the back of my mind, I kept dreams and ideas for building my own place one day too, but I'd never be far from here. In the meantime, I wanted to make sure that Cottage Row could stand the test of time.

"Well, we can certainly take a look at it all. I'm actually having dinner at the big house tonight. Anything you think I should bring? They have a favorite drink or something?" He continued, avoiding looking back at me.

"Well. I enjoy a bit of sweet tea with my whiskey. But don't worry, the liquor cabinet has been fully stocked since the fifties." I laughed. "We aren't the first kids who like a good drink." Hobie looked confused. "I'm helping Penny cook tonight, so I'll be there. You don't have to bring anything." I added.

He looked nervous, but content. I couldn't tell what that meant, but I continued.

"I think we're doing roasted vegetables, corn on the cob, and grilled chicken." I offered.

"No desert?" He asked. I glared at his false accusation with disappointment. "I'm joking." He added.

"Good save." Sticking my tongue out, "But, ice cream. It's almost always ice cream." Hobie looked my way and smiled, giving a simple nod. I was excited to have him at dinner tonight, and excited to see what he had come up with for the new irrigation system. Anything to help maintain the gardens and increase business on the property was sure to make Penny happy. It made me happy too though, seeing the way he tended to my home. I was starting to wonder if working here was more important to him than I realized, and less of just a quick paycheck. Each day that went by where he shared new ideas, and showed us how hard he works, seemed to tell me that he just might stick around a while. He had the estate's best interest at heart, and that spoke volumes about him as a man.

"Alrighty then. Tell me about your house. How big of a renovation are we talking here? What's first?" He jumped down from the fence and leaned on the post, facing me and waiting for my reply.

"Well, I was going to start small. But Port offered to pay for the renovation costs, since he'll be able to use the house down the road as a rental property. So, I kind of started over and redesigned my plans a bit. I want to start in the kitchen. I'm going to tear out the floors and the counters, paint the cabinets, and switch out the appliances. I'd really like to expand the pantry, and add some bar seating at the island, I'm just not sure there's room."

"Oh there's plenty of room." He countered.

"How can you be sure?" I asked.

"Well, let's draw it out. Let's go take a look."

"You want to draw out my new kitchen?" Though I questioned it, I enjoyed his desire to participate. I wouldn't argue the help, either. His large hands and strong arms would probably make him a good... foreman. Among other things.

"Sure. I'd be happy to. Show me." He reached up for my hand, which I took as I joined him on the ground, landing a little too close to be honest. Although, as surprising as it was, it was comfortable, right there in front of him. I can't say for sure that he agreed, but he didn't exactly work hard to back away either. I took advantage of the opportunity to look at those arms up close, arms I suddenly wanted to be wrapped up in.

I opened up the front door to my house and invited him in, kicking off my shoes on the front porch. As he walked inside, a familiar sense of home kicked in. For just a second, I almost forgot he was there to see the kitchen. It felt truly like we were returning home after a morning of work. Like we might jump in the shower, or collapse on the couch, or start to fix dinner.

Hobie followed me into the kitchen, and I watched as he looked around, studying every corner, every wall, every counter and appliance.

"This really is a beautiful house." He said.

"It is. I'm glad we didn't sell it." I jumped up onto the countertop.

"What about when you build your new house?"

"Oh, that's just a crazy dream." I blushed.

"It's a good one."

"Well, I won't let go of this place. Rent it, maybe, like Port mentioned. But I'll never let it go outside the family. Too many memories. Too much love built in these walls. I want to build more walls, for more love. I don't want to erase these."

"You're sentimental." He leaned against the counter across from me, not so subtly eyeing me up and down, in an admiring manner, not a rude one.

"Yeah, I am. Romantic movies and the bones of happy homes. What can I say? I've got a tender heart."

"I like it." His answer was short and sweet. I cleared my throat, and scooted off the counter. I didn't know what to do with the tension that creeped up on us, so I just started talking. My usual solution to problems.

"So, master of the tool shed. What would you do in a kitchen like this?" I asked.

"I'd do exactly what you mentioned, really. I'd do a giant wall of built-ins over there." He waved his hand at the far wall. "Expand the pantry right into it. Bigger refrigerator, you know, for all the kids."

"All the kids?" I laughed.

"Just a thought." He smiled, and went on. "Big stove. Like a double stove, double oven."

"More space to cook for all those kids?"

"Exactly. And I'd reframe this window here, for a better view into the backyard, a better view across the estate, right over to the water."

"Well. Keep throwing ideas like that out there and you'll have yourself a new job in no time." I suggested, impressed with his quick proposal.

"Well, let's make a list. I'd be happy to do it." He said.

"Consider yourself hired. Between you and Eddy, this place will be a dream."

"Speaking of Eddy... I told him I'd join him at the cafe for lunch. So, I have to get going."

"See, Hobie? You really are making friends. I'm impressed." I couldn't resist an opportunity to poke fun at the resident introvert.

"Just trying to say yes, now and then." He smiled like he knew I saw it, the risk he was taking: Putting himself out there, and letting himself connect.

"Well, enjoy. He's a good one."

I followed Hobie back through the house to the front door. He stepped out onto the porch, but turned and stalled before leaving.

"Ruby, I uh." But, he stopped.

"Hmm?" I replied.

"Uh, I, I guess I'll see you at dinner then." He had obviously changed his mind about whatever he was about to say, but I wasn't in a place to pry. At the very least, I finally had him considering opening up a bit. I didn't want to overdo it.

"See you then, Hobie." He nodded, and then waited a heartbeat or two before stepping off the porch. He walked across the property and back to his house, glancing back every now and then. I didn't mind the way he looked. In fact, I found that I had come to hope for it, the way he looked at me. Time seemed to skip a beat with him. It pained me a bit to admit that maybe my family was right.

I grabbed paper and a pencil, and sat down at the desk to start drawing out what Hobie had sparked in my head.

For all those kids.

It would take a lot of rooms, a lot of space, and a great big kitchen to handle *all those kids.* Honestly, I hadn't thought much about the size of my future family. I'd never really had anyone around that had me thinking about it, but there was something about the way he opened up to that conversation that had me wondering.

THE ESTATE

If I ever do get to build a place here on the estate, I wouldn't just want a house that was right for my own family. I'd want to build a place that others could call home, too. Like the big house, back when Roger and Dana lived there. Sure, it was Dana's place. But everyone knew they were always welcome, and that if you were there, you were family. It was an understood part of the deal when Port took over too, that kind of 'home' had to continue. No one would have imagined otherwise. That's the kind of house I wanted; that's the kind of home I wanted to build.

I barely got through drawing a rough sketch of the shape of a home, when I heard a knock at the door. I glanced at the foyer table, wondering what Hobie might have forgotten.

Instead, I walked into the living room and smiled when I saw uncle Eddy dropping his keys and his wallet on the same table, making himself at home, just the way I liked.

My parents were incredible, and I wouldn't trade the relationship I had with them, or with Port, for the world. But Uncle Eddy had a special place in my heart. Mom always said that after Nori passed away, Uncle Eddy dove head first into the kids lives, mine and Port's included. I was so young when she passed away, and I was still here for a few years after the rest were off to school. So, I got a lot more time with Uncle Eddy than anyone else did. My understanding of fathers and men in general was set by the example my dad and Eddy both showed me. Every kid should be so lucky. They were everything I ever thought a good human, and a good parent, and a good husband, should be. And he was the best bonus dad I ever could have asked for.

"Did I happen to see a handsome young man leaving here just a few minutes ago?" He asked, with a knowing smile.

"Not you, too." My eyes rolled so far back in my head I nearly fell over. "And wasn't he going to meet *you* for lunch?"

"Oh, of *course* me too. If someone's interested in my girl, you can be damn sure I'll need to know every single thing about him." He tapped his temple. "We old men see everything. We know everything too, you know. It's in the rules of retirement. But, being old and retired also means that no one gets to give me any hell if I show up a few minutes late. So I thought I'd squeeze in a quick visit with my favorite niece before lunch."

I laughed and joined him in the kitchen, cracking open a beer, and slipping it in a koozie before I handed it to him.

"Bless you, my child." He took a sip, gulped, and sighed with added drama. "That's a good beer. Now, I've got some ideas for getting started in here." He sat down at the island and flipped open his notebook.

I sat next to him and listened as he went through his list of ideas, floor to ceiling, room by room. It's times like these that get me sentimental. It's times like these that twenty years from now, when I'm running around this place with my own kids, I want to be able to tell them about: the days that he and I worked on this house together. When someone admires the floors, I want to remember the story. When someone can feel the history, and the love in the walls, I want to tell the stories of my years here, and the stories I grew up with. I want that kind of family history. This wasn't just a kitchen upgrade. This was a home that I wanted to ensure was solid and could hold my kids the way it held me.

"Uncle Eddy, if you could do it all again, would you do it all the same way?"

"What do you mean?" He pulled his glasses off and laid them on the counter.

"Well. Y'all had all of us kids to worry about. Do you ever regret it? Do you wish you'd done more of your own things in life?" He smiled and took a deep breath.

"You know, if I could do it all over, I'd have an even bigger family. You kids were the life of this place, and now you're carrying it on even further than we all could have imagined."

"But the chaos. The hard times. Was it ever too much?"

"It's all memories. It's what made this the place you love so much. The chaos is why you want to get this house updated, but keep the charm. It's the reason you smile when you think about that hole in the wall over there." He pointed across the kitchen to the hole I had admired before. "I think we can keep that one there, for a good story." We laughed. "The sadness... well, sweetheart, that's what makes you want to remember the good times."

"I don't ever want to let this place go, Uncle Eddy."

"I don't think you need to, baby. This place... it's in the inner fibers of your heart, you know. The estate was always here for you kids, always will be. And I know everyone's glad you're home." I slid my drawing into the silverware drawer, underneath the tray. I didn't really want anyone seeing me draw my dreams quite yet.

He wrapped an arm around my shoulders and pulled me in. "Now, about these floors."

NINE

Hobie

Each day, I'd been working on cleaning out the gardens with Penny. We'd finally gotten to a point where the old beds were cleared and ready for new soil, and the plants in-season had been weeded and trimmed back where necessary. Later that week, I walked over to meet her in our usual spot, but instead found her wrestling with some sort of wire fencing. She was frustrated, huffing and puffing, tossing the wire sheets around, and clearly losing the battle. It looked like she tried to organize different cuts of wood into different piles, too.

"I don't know exactly what it is you're working on. But it looks... well. How can I help?"

"The most helpful thing would have been to know how difficult chicken coops were *before* I ordered one. Not to mention, I ordered the grand-deluxe-larger-than-life-Ritz-Carlton type of chicken coop. You know, the big shiny comfy one, so the chickens will feel at home. Stupid chickens."

"We have chickens?" These girls kept me on my toes. I was going to have to start paying more attention around here.

"Well. I'd like to have chickens, but my dad and Rhett said I wouldn't know what to do with a chicken if it showed up on the doorstep with a basket full of it's own eggs."

"In all fairness, it looks like maybe they were right." It felt risky, taking the wrong side against a feisty one like Penny. Then again, I wasn't her husband. It couldn't be too dangerous for me.

"Well. They don't need to know that. We have to build this stupid chicken coop." She opened up the instruction booklet, but quickly tossed it to the ground. "Well. That might as well be in Russian. Hobie. Tell me you know how to build a coop." She stood with her hands on her hips, with enough frustration to burn the whole thing down.

"Tell you what. Let's go over the plans for that irrigation system real quick, and then you let me handle this chicken coop." I took the hammer from her hand like I was taking a loaded gun from a felon on the run. I mean really, she did seem pretty dangerous with a hammer. "I'll even let you tell everyone you built it yourself." She laughed and smacked my shoulder. "You sound like a big brother."

"Well. Yeah. I mean, I was. But yeah." I shook it off, not ready to get into that. I started to head over to the gardens, and Penny followed.

She spent a while showing me each section of the garden plans for the next season, and the planting and watering needs for each row. Some needed less, some needed more. They all would do better with water at different times of day, and we needed to have full control of the system so that we could shut it all down during events. It was going to be a complicated design, but once I had the plans laid out, I figured it wouldn't be too hard to actually build. I pulled my notebook from my pocket and wrote down the instructions she'd given me, along with all the ideas she had in mind for growing over the next few years. It seemed like she wanted to take a garden that was pretty to look at, and grow it enough to stock a small market. Then again, maybe she just wanted enough for the family. Come to think of it, that actually might be enough for a small market, so I figured I was about on track.

"You and this list. You have it all worked out?" She asked, peering over my notebook. "It's very old fashioned of you. I like it."

"Well, no. Not yet. But if you give me the afternoon to look at it, I'm sure I could have a good system planned out by dinner. Tomorrow morning I can go into town and start to gather what we'll need.

"Sounds good to me." She said.

"Want me to pipe the chicken coop into the irrigation system? A chicken has to drink, I think."

"Genius, Hobie. You're an actual genius." She leaned up and kissed my cheek. "You have fun with this! I have to go pick up the boys from school." She started to head back to the house.

"Oh but, Hobie. Make the water pipes for the coop on the larger side, okay?"

"How much water does a chicken need?" I asked.

"Chickens. Many chickens. No one should be alone." She winked, and it was then that I realized I was getting more than a lesson in gardening this morning. I was spending quality time with the junior matriarch of the estate, and if she was anything like the famous Dana, I'd have a lot to learn from her. Penny had everything under control. She could manage the land, the kids, her husband, and the rest of the town, as I'm sure all the ladies did before her.

And she was right. No one should be alone. Not even a chicken. Maybe not even me. Maybe things were changing, and there was hope for me yet.

I returned to the chicken coop, or rather, the pile of wood that would hopefully soon resemble a chicken coop. I set my notebook down in the grass and picked up the instructions, looking at the cover for just a second before tossing it back to its rightful place in the dirt.

"Instruction manual." I huffed. "Don't need a stupid manual."

I got to work on the coop and within about an hour, I had a sturdy home for our supposed future chickens, and my drawings for the irrigation. I washed up in time to feel the rumble in my stomach that I'd been ignoring all day. In an effort to kill two birds with one stone, I took the notebook and headed for the cafe. Food and work at the same time would get me a whole lot farther today. I hadn't exactly budgeted the time needed for a spur of the moment chicken coop. Especially if I was going to get home with enough time to clean up before dinner. I hadn't agreed to the town hall yet, but I did agree to a regular weeknight dinner with the family. The immediate family, on a school night. I figured things could only get so rowdy.

TEN

Ruby

Penny and I danced around each other in the kitchen, elbow deep in food prep. Port would usually have the grill on with a steak and some fresh catch, but he was out finishing a few things up at the marina before calling it a night. So the ladies were in charge and we brought the cooking indoors. It wasn't often that we ate what my dad referred to as "those light and fluffy girly meals" which usually involved a salad, a piece of fruit, or anything with less than ten carbs. Don't even get me started on the sugar required to make *proper* sweet tea.

In the oven, Penny was roasting a pan full of vegetables, and was whipping up her secret sauce on the stove. This sauce was known island-wide as gold; the one thing that could get kids to eat a vegetable. I was getting the chicken onto the stovetop, chopping the salad fixings, and we were brainstorming a good way to turn the corn on the cob into a cold corn salad. I found a rare lull in conversation, so I piped up and cleared my throat.

"Penny. How did you know this is what you wanted? I mean, married, kids, all of this." I gestured around us.

"Something on your mind?" She asked, sweetly accusatory.

"Can you just go with it?"

She took a deep breath, smiled, and began.

"I don't think Port and I ever had to... develop our relationship or our plans for the future either, really. The two of us just... made sense. The twins weren't exactly in the plans, at least not so soon, but that worked out. Living here, it just made sense. There was no decision making to do, if that's what you're after." She set down the sauce bowl, and started to put the lids back on everything before she returned all evidence of a recipe to the refrigerator. "Why do you ask?"

"I just... I get it. You know. People wonder what's next. But I just can't imagine planning my whole life out, especially based around a guy, which everyone around here seems to think is the most logical approach."

"Well, you don't have to. I don't think you should base your life and dreams on who you do it with. I think the right person for your life, will sort of... dream your dreams with you."

She was right. I considered her point while I chopped.

"Think out loud." She said, settling against the counter next to me, obviously ready for a sister-sister conversation.

"I think, in college, I was never really dedicated to studies or my plans because I knew my dream was here. I wasn't willing to compromise on that. So I figured, why bother anywhere else?"

"So now you're here." She agreed.

"Right. So I'm here now, doing everything I love. Where I want to be, and with my family."

"And he came along..."

"It's just that, he came here. And if he wants to stay, then yes I could let myself be very interested in Hobie. But, if this is just a stepping stone for him, I don't want to be the next step. I don't want to be someone's temporary home. This is *my* home."

"I think the perfect guy for you, the guy you're supposed to live your life with, won't find you or this place to be temporary. When you find him, he'll be the guy that wants your dreams, as much as you do."

I was so thankful to have Penny for a sister. In law, in love, whatever. She was a gift to me, and she always knew how to help me think things through. Not to mention, she was usually right. I didn't need to tell her that, though. So, I just smiled and changed the subject.

"What are you tossing into that corn?" I asked. I'd never made a corn salad, and I genuinely didn't know where she was heading with that idea.

So we spent the next hour or so fixing up the corn salad she had in mind (which was really more like a dip), getting dinner on the table, and watching the boys run all over the yard from the front porch. It wasn't too long before Hobie and Port came barreling through the door. Port was laughing about something on the shrimp boat.

"Blue wears a full life vest to this day." Port said. I assumed he'd told Hobie the story. Blue was a lucky guy. "Every day, docked or deep, he's got a full homemade five point harness style life vest strapped around him. And he still won't go on the upper deck of a boat." Hobie shook his head and sat down at the island.

"Well. Let's just hope nothing like that ever happens again." Hobie said, looking as if he wanted to change the subject.

"I suddenly feel the need to ask," Port said. "You can swim, right?"

Port's face flooded with relief when Hobie answered, "Oh yes. Don't worry about me." Satisfied, Port sat down and started to pester.

"Ladies, how are the boys? Did they break anything today?" He checks his watch. "Well.. I'll give it two more hours. What do we have going on for dinner?"

"Oh sure, I'm great." Penny kicked back. "Dinner's fluffy. You'll have to deal. Just pretend you like it and no one gets hurt."

"Fluffy?" Hobie asked.

"Usually meatless. Healthy. Fruity. Girly." Port mumbled.

"I'm going to go set the table." I saw an out from the marital bickering, and took it.

"I'll help." Hobie followed.

The twins came barreling into the kitchen, reaching right for the food. A little bit of my mom came out of my mouth faster than my brain thought it through.

"You boys get your fingers out of my dinner or you'll eat tuna salad for a week." They dropped their chips, wide-eyed.

"Sorry, Aunt Ruby."

I gave them the glare; you know, the one that says *I love you, but get out of here.*

As the boys scattered into some other form of domestic terrorism, Hobie began setting the table.

"Big kitchen then, huh?" He asked, never looking up.

"What do you mean?" I asked.

"The boys—you're so good with them. I guess you'll want a big kitchen in that dream house. You know, enough space to cook for all those kids." Finally, he looked my way, and he didn't look nearly as horrified by the conversation as I felt. I tried to shake it off.

"What makes you think I want to be the one doing the cooking?" I was sort of being sarcastic, sort of not. Maybe part of me was questioning what kind of parent he intended to be. He didn't answer, only smiled, and I continued. "Yes. I think so. A large, eat-in kitchen. Because my dining table, the real one, will probably span the entire length of a back porch, like the one here." I enjoyed this, talking about my house dreams. I'd never had anyone other than Uncle Eddy that wanted to listen.

"Ah. I'll make a note of that. Big table, on a big back porch." He walked to the cupboard, reaching for the glasses.

"Yeah. That's the only thing I'd change about dinner at the big house. When it rains, it pours, and I'd rather have a table on a covered porch, than try to squeeze everyone inside, eating standing up."

He didn't answer, instead just nodding his head, as if he agreed.

"How about you?" I pried.

"What about me?"

"Have you ever thought about your dream home? Or is it the guest house?" I joked.

"Can't say I have, really. Haven't had much reason to think about it. I've always been just fine where I am. The guest house is nice, though. Good kitchen. Short commute."

"Yeah, for a young single guy. Not for a family." Realizing my assumption, I added, "You know. If a family was in your plans."

"Hadn't thought much of it, until now."

Dinner came and went. Port complained about the fluffy meal just enough that Penny gave him dish duty.

"You should take a hint from Hobie." She said. "No complaining, no dish duty."

"Ha ha ha, I get it." Port said. "Y'all should go do something fun for a bit while the sun's still out."

"I've got to get the circus wrangled. School tomorrow. And those boys are the farthest thing from clean." Penny got up, kissed Port on the cheek, and went upstairs.

"Guess that leaves the two of you," Port suggested. "What'll it be?"

"Oh," Hobie started. "I'll probably just head back. Thanks for having me over tonight, I appreciate it." Hobie stood to leave, but something in me wasn't ready for him to go.

"How about a paddle?" I offered. Port hung his head, realizing he was missing out on some evening fun. I turned to Hobie. "Come on. You have to try it at some point."

"I uh, guess I could." His monotone was back, and I wondered if he'd reached his limits for the night.

"Maybe you can muster up some excitement." I joked, patting him on the shoulder, and stepping out the kitchen door.

"Thanks for the food, brother man." I said to Port, laying on the guilt. "Or, the cleaning I guess. I do cook a dang good meal." I rubbed my stomach as I stepped back. "Come on, Hobie. I'm going to teach you something new."

"Have fun." Port whined.

As we walked through the yard to the tower where we kept paddleboards, kayaks, surfboards, and even a canoe, I barely kept conversation going. Just enough to keep him there.

"You'll love it. Most people do. Besides, paddle boarding is the best way to watch the sunset, and burn off the weight of dinner."

"What weight?"

I gasped, looking his way to find him smiling, proud of his own joke.

"Oh. I mean if you wanted to do dishes too, all you had to do was say so." I reached to the wall and handed him a paddle.

"I'm good here." He said.

He followed my lead as we carried the boards to the water. I started us on our knees, which was an easier way to balance at first. But, he seemed to pick it up instantly, standing himself up to his feet in no time, and paddling away ahead of me.

"Were you lying about your watersport experience?" I asked, catching up to him.

"No." He laughed. "I guess I'm just a natural." I cut my paddle through the water, just for a small splash to see if he'd be thrown off. He didn't even blink. He really was a natural.

We paddled around in silence for about ten minutes, just riding the tide and enjoying the sunset, before heading back toward the house.

"You always have an audience?" Hobie asked, nodding to the house. Port and Penny were out on the back porch of the house, looking our way.

"I didn't. Not until you showed up." I said. "I think everyone around here thinks they have this novel idea of you being the prince that swoops in to save the lonely princess from her misery." I stepped off my board, a bit nervous that I'd overshared. I'd basically just opened the pages of the Ruby diaries, and welcomed him into the life and drama of a single young thing at the beach. I was blushing, so I turned away to set my paddle back into the shed.

"I'm no prince." He grunted, with a tone that sounded like his smile was long gone. He added his paddle next to mine, and then lifted our boards into the rack.

"Okay." I was a little unsure of where the conversation would go next, with his apparent frustration.

At the porch stairs, Hobie finally spoke again.

"I'm sorry. I didn't mean to be rude."

"It's okay. I'm sorry if anyone's... invading." I said, hesitantly.

"They're not. No. I just... I'm not used to people paying so much attention to me. Or my social life."

"I think that's just how our family works." I tried to brush it off. "Don't worry. I don't think it has anything to do with you." Port stepped back into the kitchen, and Hobie reached up to wave.

"I guess I'll see you tomorrow?" He asked, apologetically.

"Night, Hobie." He turned to walk to the guest house, and I stalled for a minute or two before I joined my brother in the kitchen. Part of me was eager to just head home, and avoid any awkward conversation Port had at the ready. But I had to go inside for my phone and keys at least.

As I suspected, he was waiting for me in the kitchen, perched on the kitchen island like an elf on the shelf, eating ice cream straight from the carton.

"Let it go." I said, grabbing my keys from the counter next to him.

"Didn't say a word." He took another bite. "Goodnight, Princess!"

He didn't have to say a word. I know he wondered. I did too. Hobie was... confusing. One minute he was charming and easy to be around. The next, he was standoffish, and seemed detached to us all. Still, I found my attraction to him growing deeper by the day. I needed to break in, and cross that barrier he had built up. I needed to know him better. I wanted to know everything about him.

ELEVEN

Hobie

For the first time in a long while, I woke up early in the morning the way I often have since my brother and the rest of my unit passed away: from the middle of a nightmare. Actually, being here on the estate seems to have lightened that load a bit. Not today, though.

It was rarely the kind of nightmare where things were a little sad or scary. I'd give anything to have nightmares that only bothered me a little bit. This morning was the kind I can't seem to get away from. The kind of nightmares that have me waking up in a pool of my own sweat, with my heart racing as if I've run an entire marathon. The kind where I can't figure out if I've actually been screaming, or if that was part of the dream too. On that note, looking at my knuckles, had I actually been punching something?

I'd gone long enough now feeling encouraged, like I might have finally left the darkness behind me and found what life had in store for me. But this? Waking up like this reminded me why I'd given up in the first place. Waking up like this reminded me that the darkness would never truly be gone.

My first thought was that all the family time the night before was too much. Here I was, after a simple dinner, having nightmares about losing the Dixon family, and losing this place. Not just something simple like getting fired, but truly awful nightmares. The kind that reminded me to stay away, and that everyone was safer if I just kept my distance.

A little too much fun with Ruby, a little too much of a glimpse into her future, and I was haunted all night with visions of her getting injured, going missing, or getting sick. Terrible accidents, the boys drowning. The things that plagued my brain at night were things that a normal person would consider borderline insane. For me, they were just the average concerns.

Port was still pretty adamant about taking a day, or at least a few hours here and there, for myself. I didn't understand, but was starting to realize that Port had a neverending list of work, and none of it was time pressing. So, I did the only thing I'd found could shake this feeling, and get my heart rate back in order. So I tossed on a tee shirt and some shorts, and laced up my sneakers, to head down to the pier for a run.

I sat on a bench, taking a few minutes to watch everyone on the beach. There were parents with kids, people with dogs, some people just on their own, all as if life was normal. As if I didn't just wake up not breathing.

I didn't even bother to stretch. My heart started to race again and I just took off. I ran until I reached the pier, which I knew to be at least a few miles. I slowed to a walk and continued under the pier, where I saw a group surfing. There were about twenty or so of them out there, all lined up waiting patiently. I wished I had the kind of patience and serenity that would allow me to enjoy things a bit more. I'd finally run far enough that my heartbeat settled. At the very least, I knew that feeling winded was from running, and not from having a panic induced heart attack.

I sat in the sand and took a closer look at the surfers who were closest to me. Sure enough, Ruby was out there. I wasn't quite certain at first, but the moment she paddled into a wave and popped up, I caught my breath, and I knew.

This girl, just knowing her, was going to break me. I couldn't even look at her without stumbling a bit. Now here she was, riding a wave straight into me. It actually felt like the wave was bringing her to me, and I could have sat there forever watching her just like that.

The smile across her face did it. At that exact moment, I knew that I was completely falling in love with Ruby Dixon, and I couldn't tell her. I couldn't be with her. If she knew half of the things that happened to everyone else I'd ever loved, she would run away from me. I couldn't even blame her; it would be the safest option.

Realizing that I didn't have the time or the space to get away, I stood up and took a few steps in her direction, watching as she made it the whole way in and stepped off her board. The time couldn't have gone any slower if it was frozen. Everyone behind her in the water gazed from their own boards. It was a beautiful ride, and you could tell she felt it. The glow coming off of her face right then said everything for her; this was her joy.

I waited and continued to feel my own loss. I wondered if I would ever have the friends she had. I wondered if I would ever find myself in a situation like this; in a place where I was close with someone else, maybe even with more than one person. I wondered if anyone would ever be close enough to me to notice when something brought me joy, and to celebrate that with me.

"Well hey!" she said, reaching down to pick up her board and walking toward me, knee deep in the surf.

"Good morning."

She removed the leash from her leg and sat her board down in the sand. She was standing close enough now that I could see her chest rise and fall with each breath. I caught my own breath as she flipped her head upside down and tied her long hair up. I sat back down on the sand in an effort to pull myself away. I needed to be further away from her skin. I needed to distance myself from her eyes, the ones that looked like they had never known pain. Desperate for distraction, I stared back out to the ocean, watching the rest of them wait patiently for a wave of their own.

"How are you doing this morning?" She asked, sitting next to me, painfully close. Close enough that her elbow brushed across mine, erasing the work I had just done to distance my mind a bit.

"I'm alright, how are you?" I didn't even look back to her.

"Ah, any morning out here with a nice wave or two is a good morning in my book." She leaned into my shoulder, clearly trying to get some kind of a rouse out of me.

"Looks like fun." She didn't deserve to be on the receiving end of my stress; the end where my tone was short, and my eye contact was negligible. I never should have stopped. I should have just kept running.

"What is it Hobie?" There was a sweet concern in her tone, mixed with a feeling that I might have offended her. "Last night you finally seemed like you weren't feeling tortured here. And today, you're miserable. Can you tell me what it is that has you so closed off? So back and forth?"

"I'm not closed off. I'm just, I'm—"

"Alone. Lonely. Missing something, or someone. I could count on one hand how many times you've let an honest smile across your face since you've been here."

Impulsively, I cleared my throat, stood up and brushed the sand from my hands. I had to get out of this conversation. I wanted to kiss her, and I couldn't. I wanted to tell her everything, but I didn't want to burden her. She had joy. She *was* joy. And I didn't want to take that away.

I was getting along just fine with everyone around here. Each one of them, in their own way, had an ability to take my mind off the misery I was so used to. But Ruby, in particular, didn't just clear my head in the present. She had me thinking about my future. She had me wondering what I could make of myself, rather than what I'd have to survive each day.

I wasn't one for impulse. In fact, I was mostly accustomed to feeling nothing at all, if not sadness. But this need to touch her, to be with her, it was impulsive, and I didnt want to be.

"I have to get back." It was a lie but it was the only thing that came to mind. "I'll see you later." I just took off. I ran away. From her, from my problems, from what I was afraid of. I ran away, like I always did. I ran away like a coward.

While I ran, I dove into my thoughts. I didn't move here to have the same struggles that I had before. I came here to get away from it all, from the sadness, and the panic attacks. I came here to try to find a way to make it through a day like a normal person, maybe even enjoy myself a bit. I couldn't let this happen. I was getting too close to her and to the family. I couldn't do this anymore, and it was my own fault. Everything here was going perfectly, until I started to care. Until I let them care about me. I was dangerously close to letting it all come crashing down.

I'm not sure how many miles it was to the northern tip of the island, but I got there. Before I knew it, I had run almost all the way back to the pier, and Ruby and her friends were in sight again. The sun glistened on the surface of the water, making her almost look angelic out there, just sitting on her board. She was reaching out, just touching the surface of the water.

I slowed again to a walk and just watched her as I got closer to the pier. She saw me then, and she reached up to wave. I waved back and stood still, just watching her, and trying to figure out how I was going to handle any of this; how I was going to apologize to her, and what I was going to do. She laid down and paddled herself into another wave, and just like before, it brought her right to me. If I didn't find a way to connect with her, to open up a bit, I was going to lose the first friend I made in this place.

She looked like a ballerina up there, the way she just floated along, without so much as a drift to one side or the other. She actually looked like she was flying, smooth as can be, on top of the water.

She put her board down again and stepped back up to me, hands slightly raised in front of her like I was a grenade just about to blow. I couldn't blame her.

"I'm sorry, Hobie." she said, confused.

"You don't..." I shook my head, raising my hands between us. "Don't be sorry. You didn't do anything wrong."

"Look, just... don't run away from me. Please?" She dipped her head, trying to interrupt my staring contest with the sand.

"Ruby, I can't. I moved here to just do things on my own, and stay away from everyone. I don't want to hurt you, or your family."

She reached her hand up and rested her fingertips on my chest. "What's happening here?" She asked.

"Entirely too much... and I can't put that weight on you." I laid my hand on top of hers, torn between needing her to walk away and wishing she would never let go.

"What if you could?" she asked. "What if you could just tell me whatever it is that has you hurting so badly, that you won't even let yourself make a friend here? Not even me? Could you just try to let me know you? Let me in?"

She stepped closer, dipping her head back into my line of sight again. I didn't back away, and I didn't stop her. Before I knew it, she had gotten close enough that I could feel her forehead against my chin. I could feel her breaths matching mine.

The impulse I was trying to suppress made its way through, and I kissed her. When she forced her way into my view, begging me for some kind of connection, that's how I answered her. I kissed her.

When I realized the line I had crossed and pulled away, she kept her body close to mine, only tilting her head back enough to look into my eyes. "See, you can let me in."

"No, Ruby. Please. I shouldn't have done that." I pulled her hand from my chest and took a step backward.

"Please what? Please don't care?" she asked. "I care, Hobie." She stepped into the space I had put between us.

I tucked some of her salty hair behind her ear, and realized that what I thought was blurred vision was actually tears. Tears that I didn't know I needed to cry until this moment. Tears that I hadn't cried since I moved onto the estate. And I felt those tears fall down my cheeks as I realized what I'd done—when I'd let my pain come out, my impulse take control, and my own desires impact my actions. I kissed her again. Except this time I was intentional, it wasn't just the impulse. Ruby was worth the fears I had and the tears I'd cried. I even started to think maybe she could be the one who would be safe with me, maybe even make everything worth it. Maybe she would be worth the broken road I'd stumbled on to get to her.

I held her against me and brushed my fingers through her hair, praying to God to let me kiss her like this forever, to never take her away from me. I begged Him to keep her safe. This time, as I pulled away from her, I knew for certain that she could read my mind.

"I won't go anywhere, Hobie. If you would just let me all the way in, I'll never go away. You won't lose me."

She wrapped her arms around my waist, and held onto me like she was holding on for dear life. Could she feel that in me? Could she feel the weight of it all? Could she stand it?

And I wrapped around her too, still begging God to *please, please, let me keep her.*

I pulled her hands into mine and we sat down together in the sand. I laid back and took a few deep breaths. She laid next to me, her hair falling against my face. We laid there together, shoulder to shoulder, head to head, and just breathing. She just waited for me, and it worked. All of a sudden, I was telling her everything. She waited, until I was ready. Without any warning or preparation, I just began to tell her all of it. Ready or not, here it was.

"When I was in high school, I was on the swim team. There were four of us, my relay team, who qualified for a state meet. We were all good. But, they weren't just good, they were incredible. Seriously, Olympic quality athletes, and incredible friends." She sighed out loud, and I could hear the smile across her face. It pained me, knowing I was about to ruin that.

"Well, we went to that state race, and we won. I finished two hundredths of a second ahead of the next team, and we won. I mean faster than a blink, that's all that separated us from the others. The guys all wanted to celebrate that night, but I had an AP exam the next morning. My college scholarship was academic based, it wasn't for swimming. I had to ace that test. And so I didn't go; I didn't celebrate with them. I didn't even say goodbye before we left. I just got changed, and drove home, studied a few more hours, and got to bed. Because of my stupid exam.

"Well... sometime early the next morning, maybe even late the same night, my mom woke me up, and my coach was in the living room. He'd come straight from the accident." She sat up and turned to face me.

"They died. All three of them. They died driving home. They were going the speed limit. They were all buckled. They had all just won the damn state championship, and were just excited to get home. And they got hit by a drunk old son of a bitch, and all three of them died."

I heard her catch her breath, and she reached her hand back over to my chest.

"Hobie."

"I'm not kidding when I tell you I've walked through hell, Ruby. And that was just the start of it all. People around me get hurt."

"But it was an accident. And it was so long ago. And it wasn't your fault at all."

"It was, though. I should have driven with them. We drove up there together, and I drove back with my parents. I would have taken them on the main roads to get home and they never would have gotten hit. And it wasn't just them. They were just the beginning."

"What are you talking about?" she leaned closer, and now the look on her face was going from sad, to disbelief.

"My mom. She was next."

"Well don't tell me you think that was your fault, too."

"She had cancer. And she didn't want to bother us; me and my brother. When she wasn't up to driving herself to her chemo appointments anymore, rather than asking for help, she just stopped going. She told me she was still going, on schedule and everything... and that she was doing fine. So the last two months of college I never went home to check on her. I just talked to her on the phone and took her word for it. Then one day a police officer found me and my brother on campus at lunch. He sat down at a table with us, and double checked who we were. He explained that a neighbor had called for help, and when they got there, she'd been long gone. Probably overnight at least. When we got a hold of her oncologist, we learned that she stopped going to her chemo treatments, and that he told her what would happen, but she did it anyway, because she didn't feel like she could bother us for help. And I was too busy at school to notice."

"Hobie, you're turning that into more than it is. That's awful, but it's not your fault."

"Yes, it was," I'd raised my voice, and regretted it immediately. I caught my breath before I continued. "and so was losing my brother." I was short tempered now, and I didn't want to be rude. But, I could feel my anger taking control, and I knew that when I got angry, or I started to panic, that I was never kind. And I didn't want to hurt her. I stood up and brushed the sand from my hands.

"I didn't mean to yell at you." I continued. I put my hands up between us as she stood up in front of me. "Ruby, I'm sorry. I shouldn't have yelled. I shouldn't be putting all of this on you."

"All of this? This is what's keeping you from all of us? This is what's keeping you from me? From letting me all the way in? Come on, Hobie. You're not here to just work the property and go home alone each night. Port wouldn't have hired you if he didn't think you were right for the job, and for all of us. He knew you'd be a good addition around here. It wasn't just about the work, Hobie. It's about you. He thought you would be a good fit for the property, and for our family. So stop running away from us. That's not how it works. Family is supposed to help each other with the tough stuff, not ignore it."

I took another step back from her and tried again. "Ruby. I'm sorry I haven't tried harder, but right now I might need to stick to the work. I can't get tangled up in you, or in anything else. I just need to know that I can keep a job, and keep my head above water for once in my life, and not hurt anyone in the process." I started to turn away, but turned back to her one last time.

"Ruby, I wanted you the minute I saw you, before I even knew you would be in my life every day. You spilled burning hot coffee on me and other than thinking you were a bit of a klutz, I couldn't stop thinking about how beautiful your smile was, even when you were embarrassed. I wanted to be your family the first time I watched you at the stables with the horses. I wanted to kiss you the first time I saw you drive up in your jeep listening to that god awful music on your radio. I've wanted to make you mine every single day that I've been here. But Ruby, you have no idea what you have here. Your life is perfect. Your family, your town. The way you were raised. What you have here, for the rest of your life. No one has ever threatened that. No one has left you. No one has ever done anything to ruin your life. And I'm sure as hell not going to be the one."

"That's because you *do* care. I know you do. And no, Hobie. Since you haven't let anyone in, you haven't heard about the hard stuff in this town. You haven't taken the time to learn about the year a hurricane almost wiped us off the map. You haven't been here long enough to catch Uncle Eddy sobbing at the pier, begging God to give Nori back to him." She wiped her arm across her face, to clear her tears. She bit her lip, and then stepped backward, shaking her head.

"You haven't seen Penny grow up without a mom. You haven't seen my mom try to keep her best friend's cafe from crumbling to the ground. You haven't seen my dad overcome all the pain he was dealt in the marines. I bet you didn't even know he was a marine in the first place, did you?" She was angry now. I thought I had this all figured out, that everyone and everything here was perfect. How did I miss all of this?

"And you sure haven't seen the rest of me. So don't pretend like you know I can't handle the hard stuff, like we can't handle you, or like we can't love you. Maybe if you let us walk through the hard stuff with you, maybe you'd realize that's what family is for anyway. I know you feel like you don't have a family, Hobie, but you do. If you would just let us all the way in, you would."

Whether it was my own sadness, or hers, I felt the tears fall down my face and I stared at her, unsure of what to do. I didn't know what to say, but I couldn't stand looking at her, just watching her cry, knowing I'd been the one to cause it.

"Your dad was a marine?" I was out of breath. Just listening to her raise her voice like that had my heart racing, and me desperately trying to keep my cool.

"Yes, he was. My dad got his ass kicked overseas. But you know what he did? He came home, and he figured it out. And he realized that loving my mom and Uncle Eddy and Aunt Nori made it worth it all. Worth fighting to get himself home. Worth moving on, and creating the life he always wanted despite everything that got in the way."

"I lost my brother too." I hung my head. I couldn't even look at her, telling her about another person that died because of me. "Overseas. He and the rest of my platoon got ambushed outside the gates. The only reason I wasn't there was because I forgot the dog treats that we had saved for our walk that day. I went back through the gates for some damn dog treats."

"Your brother died, and the rest of them died, and you lived. You know what that's called? That's terrible for them, and it's lucky timing for you. Maybe it's the grace of God. But it sure wasn't you, responsible for your brother's death. You weren't responsible for any of it, Hobie. You were just dealt a really crappy hand."

I didn't even know how to argue with that point. Actually, I knew that I couldn't. I knew that she was right, and that if it were anyone else I would have seen that too. But it didn't change how bad it all hurt, or how much everything felt like my fault anyway. You can only be tied to so many problems before you start to wonder if it's actually *you* causing the problems.

"But, when I came home..." she stepped toward me again. "I didn't have a family to come home to. I didn't have friends to come home to."

"And yet, here you are. You moved right into the best situation you could have ever found. You found a job that came with a family who wanted to get to know you and then decided they'd really like to love *you*, if you'd just give them the chance."

"What about you, then?" I brushed the sand from her cheeks. Her skin was salty and her hair was a mess. I stepped in, closing the gap that our back-and-forth had created. I was back where I started. Standing right in front of a girl I had been trying so hard not to fall in love with.

"What about me?" The way she looked up at me, her eyes had me completely giving in.

"Would you love me? If I gave you the chance?" I could feel her heartbeat through her chest as she pressed against me. She leaned her cheek into my hand before she answered.

"I think I already do, Hobie. I just don't know how to make you believe that, and let me." She reached to my hands, and locked her fingers in mine. The very same hands that poured me coffee in the mornings. The same fingers that showed me how to take care of the horses. The same hands that pointed me through the gardens, to different types of flowers along the trail. The very same hands that were now holding onto mine.

I didn't know it was possible to love a girl the way I loved Ruby. I think most would have said that we didn't know nearly enough about each other. We hadn't spent enough time together. We probably should have taken things a bit slower. On the other hand, I'd taken nearly thirty-four years to find her. I was starting to think that maybe that was long enough.

Forever wouldn't have been long enough, kissing her the way I did then. The way she pulled herself in closer to me showed me everything I needed to know. She might have already loved me more than anyone ever had, more than I knew you could love a person. Maybe everything I was feeling, even the fear and the what if's, was all part of how I loved her too.

"How about it then," I said, barely far enough from her that I could talk. "How do you feel now?"

"I feel like you let me all the way in," she said, resting her forehead on my chin.

"You have no idea." The world had disappeared, and it was just us and the waves.

I sat back down on the sand and pulled Ruby into my lap, her fingers tangling into my hair. When I got to the ground, she stayed right there and held on to me for quite some time. It reminded me that I had indeed let her in; all the way in.

"The backyard. Big enough for one dog? Or two?" She realized that I was referring to the drawing of the dream house, and she smiled again before answering.

"Two. No one should be alone." Penny's words came out of Ruby's mouth, and just like that I realized I'd found it. I'd found a family who knew each other inside and out. I'd found a place where one generation raised the next, and was around long enough to see them do the same. I'd found a place where hearts and souls shared the same fundamental pieces. I'd found a place where I had a chance, and maybe I didn't have to be alone.

No one should be alone.

THE ESTATE

TWELVE

Ruby

Talking on the beach turned into... *not talking* on the beach. We were already the latest story in town, and making out on the beach would have turned us into headline news. I don't think either one of us had the patience to deal with any more of that.

"How are you liking the house?" Conversation for the walk home would help to keep us distracted. I at least wanted to keep the PDA to a minimum while we were out and about.

"Well. I love it. I mean, it's a beautiful home. Just enough space to be comfortable, but not too much to take care of. Can't complain about the view, with the marina out back, and the ocean so close by. Can't really wail on the commute either." He never looked up to me that entire time.

He carried my surfboard in one arm, and kept his other hand in his pocket. Safer, probably, that we not arrive home all over each other anyway. The last thing I needed was Port watching us come up the driveway holding hands or something. My family wasn't exactly known for keeping anything on the down low. The birds would start chirping and before I know it Mayor Mallard (*yes, that's really his name*) would be shouting to the town that the little Dixon girl had finally found herself a husband. So, we were going to have to keep things subtle, no matter how much they all encouraged it in the first place.

"I loved living there, in the house you're staying in. Port said I would never have to move out, but since our old house was going to be empty, and some new ranch hand was on the way," I winked. "I figured it was time to go home. If Port wasn't going to take it, I wanted it. It's our childhood home, you know?"

"Is that the typical deal around here? Grow up, never leave, take your house back?" Hobie was still watching his feet.

"It sure seems like it. But no. Penny, Port, and I are the only ones who intend to stay on the estate. Mom and dad only have Port and me. But Eddy, he's got four kids. The twins; Ryan and Lucas, and then Jana, and then Penny."

It was a lot, and we all kind of lived like one big happy family. Especially once Penny and Port tied the knot. But when that happened it was like nothing really changed. We all knew that marriage was coming one day. Even as kids, they acted like a married couple.

"How long have they been together? The boys... they're ten, right?" he asked.

"Oh yeah. They've been together fourteen years now. But Mom and Aunt Nori used to say that they'd known it since Penny was born, that she and Port were made for each other. Then in college they actually got together and everyone went nuts. I was little though. I don't really remember the details."

"You didn't go to school with them?"

"Oh I did. Just eight years later. I'm... well you could say I was a bit of a surprise." Hobie laughed at that. "There's a reason they treat me like the baby of the family. I really am."

"You seem to love it though, having so many people to love." It finally seemed like he had an ounce or two of joy in his voice, but he still wasn't looking at me. Maybe kissing him finally loosened him up.

"It's nice. I mean, it can be hard to catch a minute alone with such a big circus running around. Don't expect anyone to keep any secrets around here. Between the boys and the broad squad, everyone knows everything, and there's not a thing you can do to get around it. Small towns have their perks, but the island wireless isn't one of them." My joking finally got him to look up.

"The island wireless?"

"Oh yes. Works at two chatty mouths per minute. I can guarantee, by the time we get home, someone will already know what happened back there."

"Ruby, what happened back there..."

"Hobie—"

"No, listen to me. Please?"

"Okay." I caved.

"What happened is... I know how you feel, and you know... you know me. You know why I just need to be here to do the job."

"And then what? More of the back and forth?" I stopped him, and turned to stand in front of him. "Then what? What are you going to do when you realize that your heart needs a heck of a lot more than a to-do list every day? All this..." I turned toward the main house and looked at it. My home. "All of this means nothing unless you have people to share it with, and I don't mean the workload, Hobie. I mean the good days, and the bad ones. Someone who can celebrate with you when you ride your first wave without falling off. Someone who can hold your hand when Sampson over there breaks your toes."

He laughed at me. "Ruby."

"Give it time. He's old but he's still a menace."

"Ruby."

"I'm not finished."

"You're cute when you're feisty."

THIRTEEN

Hobie

"Still talking." She smiled and raised her finger to my face. "None of this matters, Hobie. You can live in that pretty little house for the rest of your life. Feed horses, manage a garden, help at the cafe, drive your old truck, and have your little silent party for dinner every single day. And one day you're going to open your eyes and realize that you missed everyone that was right here the whole time, right in front of you."

"I've never missed you, Ruby. Not once. It's taken everything I have to stay away from you, and let you walk away."

"Then stop it. Stop letting me walk away. And God, Hobie, what if you stopped running away from me, too?"

When I didn't answer her right away she got nervous. I could see her breathing faster. Then, after a few seconds of silence, it was almost as if we'd said everything we needed to say, and we were satisfied with the conversation.

I was going to kiss her again. I'd been doing my best to keep myself under control for the whole walk home. But she beat me to it, lunging at me, slamming into my chest; which seemed part in lust and part in anger. Whatever it was, I welcomed it. If this was how she kissed when she was angry then I was ready to solve all kinds of disagreements. She was back where she belonged. I could feel it in my bones that this girl was created to be right here with me, attached to me with her hands around my back, her toes on mine, and her hair just underneath my nose.

"I don't want to lose you, Ruby. I don't have it in me. I won't make it through that kind of darkness again. I can't."

"Well then let me be the boss of that. You're not going to lose me, or anyone here, Hobie. Please, just—"

I stopped her rambling with another kiss. This time was different. This time I wouldn't stop. She was mine and I was hers, and no matter what it took, I was going to learn to live with her, in her, surrounded by her, and tangled up. No matter what my head said about the danger, about the possibilities of this ruining me, ruining everything. Our lives collided here, regardless of the paths we took along the way. Maybe love has a way of finding you through your mess. I was going to figure out a way to love her and keep her safe at the same time.

"Just what?" I pulled back, and smiled.

"Just, that." She cleared her throat, and wiped her thumb across her bottom lip. "That's all."

I brushed her hair out of her face, and kissed her nose.

"Alright, then." I looked over to the house, to the two rocking chairs on my front porch that suddenly seemed like they had been telling me all along.

"Would you please come to dinner tonight?" She begged. Loving her was going to hurt, and have me doing things I swore I wouldn't. Loving her was going to have me completely out of my own control. Loving her meant being in her control. That, I was sure of.

"I'll think about it."

"Great. Dad usually lights the grill around six, but the kids will be playing basketball in the driveway as soon as they get home from school, so you can head over there any time. I have to go help close up the cafe, so I'll see you at the house later."

"Ruby, I said I'd think about it." This girl was going to drive me nuts.

"See you there." She kissed me on the cheek and walked away, and it was almost painful. I knew she needed to get changed and head to the cafe, and I wouldn't have minded helping her.

I twisted the top off a beer before collapsing into the rocking chair on my front porch. I'd managed to keep myself occupied around the property for the rest of the day, but as I settled back in, the ideas of home and family, and even friends, began to weigh heavily. I sat for a few minutes to absorb the noise: the cars in the driveway, splashing from the pool. The chaos of it all. I'd done pretty well avoiding that mess so far, but if

I didn't go to dinner tonight, it was safe to bet that she'd end up over here beating my door down. Lord knows nothing good would come from pissing off a spitfire like her; except maybe making up. But I'd never live it down.

I stepped inside to grab my shoes and hat, and returned to the front porch to find exactly what I'd expected. Ruby, standing there, arms crossed across her chest, looking ready for a tussle.

"So you haven't backed out." She said.

"If I wasn't coming, I'd have been long gone by now." Truthfully, I was running through ways to disappear now anyway.

"Well, then." She reached her hand out to me. "Let's go."

I was going to that dinner whether I wanted to or not. I also wanted to take advantage of another minute or so here in the house, just the two of us, and I did.

"You don't have to be nervous, you know. You already know everyone here." We walked through the yard together, close but with enough distance that we wouldn't spark any chatter. I even kept my hands in my pockets.

She tried to let the flush fall from her cheeks before we left my house, but I could still tell. Not that I was complaining. I wouldn't mind looking at her all through dinner, knowing that she was thinking about my lips on hers.

"It's not about meeting new people." I said. It really was hard to explain. "I just haven't been social, really, in... well, it's been years since I put any work into relationships. I'm not good at small talk. I'm not very entertaining, and I'm not usually someone that people are... Well let's just say no one's been eager to be around me either."

"Give it time," Her confidence was enough for the both of us. It made me wonder if she truly understood, if she ever could. "and maybe, oh I don't know. Try to put a little variety in your tone? Try sounding like you actually want to be here?" She winked at me.

"You mean you don't want the King of Monotony?" She didn't find it as funny as I did.

By the time we got there, the basketball game had ended and the adults had all moved to the kitchen. Rhett was manning the grill on the back porch and people flowed in and out of doors all throughout the house. I followed Ruby inside where I found Port digging into a bowl full of pasta salad. Eating here just a few days ago was a great time when it was only the four of us and the kids, but with the whole town here, this place didn't feel quite right. There was no rest, no calm. The kitchen that we relaxed in before suddenly felt like a prison.

Maybe this was where healing began. Maybe I needed to feel the urge to leave, and choose to stay. Maybe this was my shot at growing past all of this, at having a normal life.

"Did you make that?" I choked out, to Port.

"I sure didn't. Uncle Eddy handles the pasta salad. Better get some, there won't be any leftovers." He said most of that with his mouth full.

"Hobie," Penny was sing-songy with surprise. "It's great to have you here." She leaned into my ribs for a hug. "It's about time you took a break and had some fun." She handed me a plate and a glass, pointing to a pitcher on the countertop. "I'll let you pour your own. You better make it quick though; Ruth will be all over you in a few minutes asking how you like it."

I began to pour and cracked a smile when I saw the pink fill my cup. "That's the most lady looking drink I've ever poured." I said, taking a sniff. "What exactly am I drinking here?"

"Officially? Pink Sea Salt. Grandma Ruth makes it, although we're pretty sure the alcohol content has increased gradually over the years. Apparently it's a family recipe. No one is quite sure what's in it though, so just keep it to a half glass, and you'll probably live." Ruby winked.

"Oh, don't be a lightweight." I recognized the shaky voice. Penny choked on her drink and covered her mouth as she laughed. Wit and sarcasm ran generations deep around here. I turned to see Ruth leaning on her cane as she made her way into the kitchen.

"I don't think Hobie's a lightweight, Ruth." Port said, mouth still full.

"Never know." I said. "I might surprise you." I was trying my hardest to engage in the conversation like she asked, making attempts to be the King-Of-Not-Monotony. Although, I really did need to make more of an effort to cut back on the damaging habits. Painkillers and alcohol served me well in the past, but I had new ideas about the future. None of them involved bad

THE ESTATE

habits. For now, a drink at dinner couldn't hurt. I'd done just fine
so far with a beer at dinner. But no, I didn't want to go proving
how much I could handle.

I already knew we all got along, but I wanted to enjoy this
dinner with them, and I wanted Ruby to know that I really was
trying. I was so used to standing in the corner, or avoiding parties
at all. If I was going to give it a shot, I was going to have to be all
in.

The conversation continued around the kitchen island as
some snacked, some cooked, some drank, and others drank some
more. The kids came running in and promptly got kicked out. It
worked though, the ebb and flow, and being in the middle of it
all. Of course, I watched my steps. I let the crowd settle before I
got any food. I stayed behind the main circle of everyone gathered
shoulder to shoulder. It was all I could do to make it feel bearable.
At least, I thought it was a good start.

Rhett peered through the doorway and said something,
leading Eddy out of the kitchen off the porch. I watched through
the window as they walked out toward the gardens. Other than
my brother, I'd never had a friend like that. Other than my mom,
I'd never had anyone that interacted with me the way they all did.
The love, the joking, the guiding conversations full of loving
criticism and honest advice. I was almost starting to relax in the
hum of everyone having a great time when I felt it.

In a way it felt like I had been struck by lightning. Or,
maybe someone had kicked me in the back. My ears were ringing
and my stomach turned. My head felt like cement. I felt the glass

slice my hand. Not once, not a scratch. It was more like slices, stabbing, and throbbing pain. The voices around me had gone silent, and instead I heard a muffled noise; the kind that sounded like you were underwater. I felt like I was stuck in a blink. Everything was dark and hot, like my skin was on fire.

Ruby wrapped a towel around my hand, standing in front of me, trying to tell me something, but I didn't hear. Penny was behind her, shuffling everyone out of the kitchen.

Port pulled his phone up to his ear. "Stop—" I heard.

"Hobie... hand." I heard her voice again, and looked back down to Ruby. "Hobie."

"I uh, I need to go." I mumbled. "I'm just, I think I—" I pulled my hand away from Ruby and stumbled as I tried to step toward the back door. My head was running through the fastest way out. From here to my front door. From here to silence. Away from everything. What was happening to me? I only made it a few steps through the kitchen

"Hobie." I looked to my right, and Port had a hand on my shoulder, and the other reached out in front of him. Instinctively, I threw my arm up between us, but he was quick to grab my wrist, and slowly lowered my fist back down. "It's okay, Hobie. It was just my dad and Eddy. They took the guns out to the field. It's okay."

I didn't answer, I don't think. I just watched the ground fly by as I ran back to my house. I just had to get out of it all, and this would stop. If I could just get back inside, everything would stop. If I took a cold shower, maybe I could shock my system into working order. Maybe I could clear the fog that had taken over my head.

I jumped over the steps up to the porch, and pushed through my front door, across the house and to the kitchen sink. I hit the faucet hard enough that the water started spraying from the side. I held my hand under the cool water until I heard her voice again behind me.

"It's just me, Hobie." She was basically whispering. "Can I help you?" I counted her footsteps as she walked across the house. By now I knew each creak in the floors. So it didn't startle me when I felt her hand on my shoulder blade, I knew exactly where she was.

"Let me help you." She said quietly, again, reaching for my hand in the sink with a clean towel. She rewrapped it tightly with another kitchen towel, and then reached to turn off the kitchen sink.

"I think I broke it." I looked at the faucet.

"Port can fix it. Don't worry about that." She answered. "Can we sit? Please?" She pulled me into the living room.

I could still feel my heartbeat hard enough that I couldn't tell where one beat stopped and another started. I followed her to the couch, leaned my head back, and caught a quick glimpse through the window of the dinner party that had continued with everyone gathering outside. It served as a reminder that not everyone was so weak and traumatized that a sudden loud noise sent them running. Most of them had sat down at the table to eat now, but Port was standing on the edge closest to us, just watching. Rhett and Eddy walked up to him at the stairs to the porch, shotguns resting over their shoulders.

"I'm sorry." I said, hanging my head. "I don't know what happened."

"I know exactly what happened." Ruby answered. "Dad and Eddy went out to the edge of the gardens for target practice. Pretty normal thing, I guess... if you aren't dealing with PTSD."

"Maybe."

"Hobie, we probably need to take you to the hospital, and make sure they get all of the glass out of your hand."

"I'm fine."

"You are not fine. Not at all."

"I told you. I warned you. I'm a mess. You don't want anything to do with this. Trust me."

"You know that isn't going to work." Ruby stood up from the couch and sat on the coffee table in front of me.

"Your brother won't mind getting rid of me when he realizes that I'm no good for you." I said. "He couldn't possibly want a short fuse like me working here, ready to blow at any time. Maybe I should go." I could feel my little bit of progress unraveling.

"I think he's just worried. He doesn't know anything about what you told me, Hobie, but he grew up with the same dad I did. He does know panic when he sees it; and we saw it. He's just going to want to help. That's just Port, it's what he does. He's good at fixing things."

"I can feel the glass in my hand." I looked down at the towel, and saw the blood soaking through.

"Please let me take you to the hospital." She begged.

Right as I was about to agree, I heard the truck door open and shut. Port appeared at the door a few seconds later.

"Hey man." He said, without walking up to join us. "Let me take you to the hospital. Let's get this fixed up real quick."

I looked back to Ruby, and she just smiled and nodded. "Why don't y'all go. I'll go help with dinner."

I wasn't sure if I was ready to be on my own with Port, having to explain what had happened. I knew it would lead into a deeper conversation; one that I wasn't sure I was ready to have with anyone else. I was still kind of amazed that I'd said as much as I had to Ruby. Then again, with her the words flowed so easily, I barely had time to second guess what I was doing. She must have known that it was a good time for a reminder.

"And Hobie." I stopped at the bottom of the porch steps and turned to face her. "I'm glad you came tonight. It won't always end like this."

"Maybe." I looked to Port, who seemed to understand that there was more to the conversation. I knew she was right.

"I'm proud of you." She added.

"Glories of a small town. Nothing's all that far away." Port laughed as he parked the truck in the hospital parking lot, just a few minutes after we left the house. I hopped out and followed him inside. Through the sliding doors, Port walked up to the front desk.

"My man! What happened buddy? You already trying to take out the new guy?" The man at the desk obviously knew Port well. Not that I was surprised.

"Very funny, Doc. Look. Hobie here got into a bit of a disagreement with a glass. Can you get him taken care of?"

"Sure thing, Dixon." The man grabbed a clipboard with some paperwork on it and then led me to a triage bed behind that desk. "Alright, have a seat." He went to hand me the clipboard and a pen, but quickly realized that wouldn't work.

"Dixon! Get over here." Port came over from the lounge and sat on the countertop. "Make yourself useful and fill this out for your buddy here. I'd venture a guess that... his hand hurts."

We spent the next two and a half hours getting the glass cleaned out of my palm and wrist, and stitches put in. Thankfully Dr. Malone felt confident that it was just a "stitch and fix". Nothing deep enough that he'd send me to get tendons repaired and other pieces put back together. As soon as the stitches came out I'd be good as new. He only asked that I drop by in a few weeks so he could double check the healing, which I was happy to do, knowing that my workload mostly required the use of two strong hands. That is, if I still had a job. I wouldn't blame Port if he used this as a reason to find someone else for the place.

Dr. Malone mostly worked through small talk and banter with Port. But at one point, with Port distracted by a candy bucket at the desk, Doc looked up and took a deeper look at a couple of my visible tattoos, hesitating to speak.

"Go ahead, sir." I suggested.

"Well, Hobie. I don't mean to imply that I know where you come from or what's going on in that head of yours. But, I figured I'd let you know. If you stick around long enough and think you're up for it, a good buddy of mine, McGraw, is a psychiatrist. When he retired from the Navy, he went back to school and has been working with veterans ever since." He continued his stitching.

"How'd you know?" I asked.

"Small town, bud. And the tattoos helped." He never looked up, just kept working. "Anyway, McGraw's a good guy. A few more guys came out of some bases not too far from here, and now he's got himself a nice group that meets each week. All sorts of guys. Navy, Army, Marines?" That's when he looked up.

"Yes, sir."

"Well, they don't sit in a circle and sing kumbaya. McGraw usually has his guys out doing something. Fishing, surfing, trips up to a cabin in Blowing Rock. Hell, they even went skydiving last month. He's a wild son of a bitch, but I like the job security he provides." He laughed, still staring at his stitching.

"So. Just wanted to put that out there. Whenever you find yourself ready to work on something, there's a place for you to go. Maybe, feel a bit more relaxed when you're holding a glass."

"Thank you, sir. I'll keep that in mind."

As Doc cleaned up the space where he put my mangled hand back together, Port finished up his social time with everyone at the desk. That seemed like his nature anyway, but it also served as a reminder of my new residence in this small town. The more of it I saw, the more I saw the opportunity to have a life I'd never had before. It seemed like maybe Ruby was right, that maybe friends can be family if you let them. Everyone here sure treated Port like family, and me too, seemingly by default. In the parking lot, Port ran the back of his hand across his forehead, adjusting his hat. He leaned on the edge of the truck bed across from me, with caution, before he spoke.

"Listen man. I'm not going to pry. I figure you'll say and do whatever you're comfortable with. I just want you to know that... you don't have to keep anything from us or from me. If something's tough on you, or bothering you, well... if I can't help you out, there's always my dad or Uncle Eddy. No one in my family is all that good at leaving people alone, and I think between the three of us, we're pretty good for handling almost anything that could be going on. So, I just wanted you to know. Whatever it is, you don't have to figure it out alone."

"Thank you." I knew I was going to have to have this conversation with him at some point. I just figured that after a few pain pills probably wasn't the best timing.

"And uh, for what it's worth," he continued. "Ruby, she's like a cannon. She's got opinions, attitude, jokes, and the energy of a toddler loose in Disney, pretty much all the time. But she's a good listener... and she's got this incredible patience and grace that I've never seen in anyone else. So, well. I just thought I'd mention it."

"Thank you. I appreciate that." It was pretty clear that this part wasn't about getting me to talk. That was Port letting me know that whatever happened between me and his sister, that he was on board, which led me to believe that maybe my job was still safe too. It seemed to me like he was a bit hopeful, encouraging, even. It made me wonder what she'd told him, or any of them.

We pulled through the property gates, and down the driveway I saw Ruby step out onto her back porch. She waved, and I lifted my fingers from the window to wave back.

Tonight was a mess. In my own head it felt like five steps backward. But maybe, when it came to everyone else I'd taken a step forward.

THE ESTATE

FOURTEEN

Hobie

The following week was deemed "vacation" by Penny and Port. They spared me the embarrassment and told everyone at dinner that I dropped a glass and tried to catch it, leaving the depth of that night to a small circle. I was told to take the week and get some fresh air and relax, but I spent the first four days in the house, avoiding everyone and anything.

Mostly, I slept. I ate a bit. I questioned my choices, moving here to the estate, and still being here. The initial pain and swelling had faded, and I was left with mostly just a constant itchy bruised feeling in my hand.

Since dinner, Ruby and I had talked on the phone each night. She left town the following morning to head out to the farm in Kentucky where she was taking a look at a few horses that she was hoping to adopt and bring back to the estate around Christmas.

Port stopped by once each day, just to see if I needed anything. I usually told him that I was just sleeping and that the pain meds kept me pretty relaxed. It was true, I just left out the part where I was taking a bit more than the prescription suggested. Old habits die hard, and this one reared an ugly face at the very first opportunity. I did what I could to keep everyone away until Friday night, when Ruby showed up on my doorstep. Her knock was light, and patient.

"Hey." I opened the door, leaving her on one side of the screen, and me on the other.

"Hi." She said, smiling. She glanced down at my hand and then back to my eyes. She didn't look at me with pity, and I appreciated that. I pushed the screen door open toward her, and she stepped inside.

"How was your trip?" I asked, leading her to the kitchen, watching as she climbed up to the bar stool at the island and sat down. She began to pick grapes from the bowl of fruit and sandwiches Penny had dropped off.

"It was good. Quiet though. Maybe next time you can come with me." Watching her eat grapes was more enjoyable than it needed to be, and I didn't know what to do with something so stupid and simple like that.

"I don't know much about rehoming horses." I put a coffee mug in front of her, and poured her a cup. It was all I had to offer. I hadn't really been eating much this week, which she probably guessed from the full basket of food on the counter.

175

"I handled the horses on my own. I just..." She paused, adding cream to her coffee. "I missed you, Hobie." I dropped my head, unsure of what to say, or rather, how much to tell her.

I missed her so much it was painful. It was as if I could feel her absence in my lungs, every time I tried to take a deep breath. It felt like every mile away she was, was another shard of glass through my hand. She was all I thought about when I was awake, and all I dreamed about when I was asleep; but did I need to tell her all of that? Was that a wise step forward? What was really going on here?

"Say something, Hobie." Her voice shook, and whether I was overreacting or not, it felt more like a lack of confidence in me than in the conversation. I didn't know where we left off, really. I just knew how I felt.

"I missed you too, Ruby. Every day." She got up from the island and walked around to stand in front of me. She leaned in close, her chest against mine and her hands on my waist. I reached up to play with her hair. I'd missed her long dirty blonde hair, watching it fall over her shoulders. I'd missed watching her braid it before getting to work in the stables. It had only been a few days, but I had missed everything about her. Things had changed enough now that being alone felt wrong, and being with her felt right.

She didn't say anything else, only leaning her cheek into my hand. She seemed to enjoy resting her head in my hands, and I'd come to love holding her. I hesitated, knowing exactly what I needed to tell her, but was afraid to say.

"Whatever it is, just say it. Stop holding things back from me."

"I love you, Ruby." With the words finally out of my mouth, I felt like I'd taken the breath that had been held from me since the day she left. When she smiled at me, I scooped her up and carried her across the house, collapsing into my bed. As we settled, she answered me.

"I love you too, Hobie." She sounded like heaven, whispering beneath me. Rather than wonder, now I knew. Rather than hope, I could feel it in my soul. She loved me, and I loved her, and for just a moment, that was the only thing that mattered.

I could have looked at her there beside me forever. Our breaths matched, and she was closer to me than she had ever been before. She brought her hands up to my shoulders, and looked away from my eyes. A shyness took over her; it was like my Ruby went away.

"Hobie." She whispered, as her hands took a tighter grip on me. Tracing my thumb across her cheek, I realized that I'd never seen this shy side of her before. I wasn't sure what to do with it, so I just held her closer.

"Where'd you go?" I touched my nose to hers.

"Hobie, you should know that I, uh..." The tension in her words was unbearable. I tried to lift her chin to get her back to me.

"Look at me." I said.

"I haven't, uh... Hobie. I just..." Her eyes watered and her cheeks blushed. I touched the corner of her eye, wiping away the tear that sneaked it's way out.

"How can I make you happy?" I asked, smiling. I knew that it didn't matter what happened right now. I loved her. If all I did for the rest of time was hold her, and kiss her, I'd be the luckiest man alive. Not a single ounce of me wanted anything more. If she didn't want me, or wasn't ready, then neither was I. If I was going to be the first and the only, and I was, then it was going to be perfect. I was going to love that girl more than she knew was even possible.

"I want everything with you." She whispered.

"Eventually, sure. One day." It worked, and she smiled. "You just tell me what we're doing here, whatever it is. Because I'd be happy to go scoop us a couple bowls of ice cream and start that movie you love so much." The apprehension finally faded from her face as she smiled at me, and I hoped that meant that she didn't feel worried about us anymore. She didn't need to. How I felt about her had nothing to do with what we would or would not end up doing.

"I love you." I said. "I just want to love you." She smiled again, and I felt her come back to me. Her stress gone, her grip on my back loosened as she drew her hands over my shoulder blades and down my arms. I dried the last tear from her eye, silently vowing to never be the reason she cried.

"I knew you were strong," she said. "but you're gentle, too."

"I don't have to be." I whispered, which made her giggle. Mission accomplished. Her laughter could solve any problem. I understood her the way I always hoped I would understand someone. All I needed was to look into her eyes, and I'd know how she felt. She'd never need to find the words with me. I just knew.

She was perfect. She was the most beautiful person I had ever seen, and she had no idea. She certainly didn't realize that I found her beauty to be equal, inside and out.

"You are absolutely perfect." I said.

"You don't know that."

"Don't worry. I'll show you."

So, I did. I held her close for the rest of the night, making certain that she felt safe, and wanted, and at home here with me. I never did let go of her. Just shy of falling asleep, I rolled onto my back, and pulled her with me. She settled into the space beside me, leaned her head onto my chest, and listened to my heart rate slow.

"Hobie?"

"Mhm?" I kissed her forehead. Laying there together turned into at least a few hours of well deserved sleep.

"I just... don't want you to think..."

"It doesn't matter what anyone thinks, Ruby. You're stronger than that. But, I think you're exactly right for me. That's all that matters." I hadn't been in a position to boost someone up in a long time. If anything, I was the one who'd been carried. But

179

she put her heart in my hands, and for the first time I felt like someone was trusting me, depending on me. I mattered to another person, and that carried a weight that had the potential to turn my life around. It already was.

I understood then, what it meant to be designed for one woman. I was certain that I'd never fit so perfectly with another human being for the rest of my life. She was made for me, and I for her.

When she fell asleep again, I snuck out into the kitchen for some water and a snack, intentionally taking only the suggested dose of pain pills for my hand. She deserved better than that, better than the choices I'd made in the past. She deserved a man who made the best choices for himself, and created a safe environment for her. Loving her meant taking care of myself, too.

I was going to tell her about the pills, and about before. But if I was going to be good for her, the best for her, I was going to start now. I'd start by taking a prescription medication the way it was prescribed. Sounds simple, but it was bold.

I was barely gone a minute before she joined me in the kitchen, wrapping her arms around my stomach from behind me. I spun around to face her and pulled her as tight as I could without squishing the insides right out of her. Never, as long as I lived, would I be able to get close enough to her. I'd never been one to need this kind of closeness. I'd neer needed to be hugged. I survived just fine on handshakes and salutes for so long. But now that I knew her, it was like touching her was all I'd ever needed. Being close to her calmed my racing heart, and my anxious mind.

"How's my girl?" I asked.

"Never better." She looked up smiling, and I kissed her cheek.

"I can't imagine what you must think of me." she said.

"What are you talking about?"

"I know I'm usually so... outgoing and loud."

"I think it's confidence. And it looks good on you." I winked.

"So you don't think the quiet side of me is silly?"

"I don't think you're silly," I answered. "I think... you're beautiful, strong, and strong willed. You're smart, and kind of a smartass." She smacked my shoulder when I laughed. "Ruby, you make me relax, in a way I haven't in years, or maybe ever. You breathe out and it's like I can breathe in again. I can't tell you the last time I felt that way, like I could really just breathe. You're my air, Ruby. I didn't really know the feeling before, but here with you, I feel like I am home for the first time. So, you can stay here or not. Whatever you want to do, we'll do. It isn't going to change all of that."

Relief looked a lot like a smile on her. A man like me, with the history I've got, doesn't love quickly and doesn't love easily. I'd spend the rest of my life making sure she understood what she had accomplished, and the gravity of it; making me love her. I loved her fiercely, but the rest of that night I loved her softly. I loved her carefully, and slowly. I loved her in a way that made clear that she was a gift, and that I knew I would never deserve her. I loved her enough to show her that I would always treasure her, and take care of her. By morning, I was confident that she knew.

Honestly, by the morning, even I was surprised at how much had changed in just one night. Sure, we had our fun, but we also did a lot of talking. This time, we didn't get stuck in anything from the past. Instead, we talked about hopes and dreams for the future; all those kids that would fit in that house. The most amazing part about it was that lying there with Ruby was the first time I'd really considered hopes and dreams for myself. Ruby and her family and her home had opened my eyes to the idea that the future might have me in it. Not long after falling asleep again, my phone rang. I pulled my arm away from our tangle to answer it.

"Morning, Port. What's up?"

"Hey man. I need to get something out to the Erv. I wanted to see if you were up for a trip. I know I had said take a week, and it hasn't quite been, so if you need to hang out this morning, I totally understand. I was just thinking about you, and thought I'd check in."

I looked at Ruby, still asleep, and smiled. There was a peace about us already, and I knew I didn't have to worry about leaving her. I knew she would be there when I got back, or that she would come back to me again. This wasn't a one time deal; she wasn't a one time kind of girl. She was the everyday and forever type.

"Sure, no problem. I'll meet you down at the boat in ten minutes." I set the phone back on the nightstand, and eased myself the rest of the way out of my knot with Ruby, and left her sleeping there in my bed; making sure, of course, that she was properly tucked in and warm before I left. I got dressed as quietly as I could, and snuck out.

Port was passing through the yard to the marina as I stepped off the porch. He was carrying an overloaded crate full of brown bag lunches.

"What's in there?" I asked, realizing it was a bit nosy.

"Oh Penny couldn't sleep last night. Spent about eight hours baking. So, I'm offloading some of it to the guys. I can't eat all this by myself. Don't worry, I packed you a bag too. I tried to take one over to Ruby, but she isn't home. Isn't at the cafe either, so... her loss." He laughed.

"Well, I take my desserts very seriously. If she isn't around to claim hers, I'll gladly take it." I joked, hoping I could hide that I knew where she was.

"There's a little more sunshine in your mood today, man. What's got you so chipper?" He asked. I obviously wasn't about to tell him that I had just spent the night in bed with his sister. No matter how clear he was about his approval of our spending time together, there was not a single part of last night that needed to be shared with him. Either way, that wasn't my conversation to have. That would be entirely up to Ruby, if and when she decided there was something to share.

"Just, finally feeling rested, that's all. Thank you, for bringing me here. I know you just gave me a job, but I kind of feel like I am getting my life back too."

As we stepped onto the boat, he hesitated for a second before speaking again.

"Hobie, listen. I know I probably prodded too much at the hospital last week. But, this morning, I've just been thinking. I want to make sure that you..." He reached up and pulled his hand down his beard a few times, clearly struggling to find the right words. "I need to make sure that we're all... that you feel safe here. I want you to feel safe here on the property, and with everyone else around you."

"Port..." The truth was, other than the surprise at dinner last week, I really was starting to feel settled here.

"No, Hobie. I understand that you're working through a lot, and that's not your fault, that's not even a problem. That's just life. You've been a really good addition to the estate, and I just want to make sure that we're doing everything we can to really make this place feel like home for you. This isn't just a job, Hobie. You're a part of our team, and I want you to feel like it, moving forward. I want you to feel comfortable, and let us walk through life with you, whatever it is that you're walking through. I'm glad you feel like you're getting your life back, and I'll try not to pester you about it anymore. I just want you to know that here, living here with us, you don't have to worry about your future."

I took a breath, absorbing everything he said. He sounded like a friend. He sounded like a brother. I appreciated it, and I wanted to store this feeling in my soul.

"Port. I think this is exactly where I need to be. I have a lot of learning to do, or maybe unlearning, depending on how you look at it. I've walked through a lot of dark places over the years, and I'm kind of... just starting to feel like I'm worth the time it takes to fix it. I'm sorry if it's affected you at all. I don't want to add any stress to your plate. I just want to make sure I'm as much help as I can be. I want to be worth the hire. Y'all have a lot to offer, and I want to make sure I earn it. I'm sorry I let my personal life get in the way." Even though talking to Port was a painful reminder of losing my own brother, it was also a glimpse into the possibility of moving forward. Maybe family wasn't just something I'd lost anymore. Maybe there was family to be found.

"You didn't let your personal life get in the way, man. It was a personal dinner. With personal friends. Eating together like a real family does. That had nothing to do with work, but instead everything to do with you as a person, not you as an employee. And look, work aside, I want to know that I'll do anything I can, as a friend, to keep you here. To keep you going. Everybody needs that sometimes, right?"

"Thank you, Port." I reached out to shake his hand, but as a real friend, or a brother, probably would have, he pulled me in for a hug. The old fashioned, shoulder slapping, honest to God, hug. Just like Ruby, Port was reminding me that I'd found a life here. Not just a job. Not just people I could lose, but a whole life. Work, friendship, hobbies, faith to fall back on, and... a future.

I saw Ruby walking across the lawn and toward the marina. I nodded in her direction, and Port turned around to see.

"Morning!" he shouted, before turning back to me with a knowing look on his face. Not skeptical, not concerned; he just knew.

"Morning Hobie," she smiled as she got closer. "Big brother. Slash boss man. Hobster here needs the morning off."

"I do?" I asked, confused.

"He does." She just winked at me before continuing in whatever argument she had planned for Port.

"I'm not even going to ask." Port said. "Look, get that crate over to the Erv, and then the day is yours. Just be careful, huh? I don't need to lose the only quality help I have around here."

"That's painful." Ruby snickered, dramatically slapping her hand to her chest. "As if I don't run this place."

"You wish." Port stepped up onto the dock, and turned toward the house, leaving Ruby and I alone on the boat. "Good talk. Later guys!"

The ride out to the Erv was a peaceful coast. She took the crate up onto the deck, quickly handed out the bags to the guys and then stepped back down. I reached to hold her hand to help her back onto the boat.

"Well would you look at that. Beauty and the beast out together this morning." Stewart leaned over the Erv and cracked a smile as he spoke.

"Just working, Stew." Ruby said.

"Now look. My wife would have my tail if I didn't at least take the opportunity to encourage this... well. Whatever it is you have going on here."

I hung my head with a smile and tried my best to stay out of it. This was her town, and her business. It wasn't my place to interfere.

"Thanks, Stew. I'll be sure to let Chelsea..." She looked back up to the boat at the rest of the guys all hovering, and a feisty smile crossed her face.

Uh oh.

"You know what?" Hands to her hips, I could almost feel her fire light up. "Why don't all you Nosy Nellies tell all of your wondering wives that sweet single Ruby is doing just fine on her own, and doesn't need the whole married herd to meddle."

"They's meddlin' because they love you, sweetheart." Hugo interrupted.

"Well quit meddling and get back to work." She waved her hand at the guys. "And don't eat all that in one sitting. Most of y'all are riding on the line of diabetes as it is." I bit my lip to silence my laugh. "Maybe you should drink a bottle of water while you're at it. Eat some lettuce or something." She stomped back over to the wheel and hit the gas so hard I thought the boat was going to flip over backward.

"Hell, Ruby. Who are you racing?" I pulled myself up onto the captain's chair and held on tight. She was bound and determined to get us wherever she was going as fast as possible.

"I just hate that. I have a brother. I don't need eight more." She said, letting off the throttle a bit.

"They're just picking." I smiled. "Can't say I mind someone else pointing out that you and I look good together." I wrapped around her while she drove, kissing her neck.

"Is that the idea then?" She asked.

"What do you mean?" I asked as she slowed the boat to a mild pace and turned around to face me. "Ruby, listen. Whatever this is, the only thing I know is that you don't seem like the type to run away. So, if you're trying to give me a chance. Maybe…"

"Maybe you'll quit trying to live life on your own, and maybe let me live it with you?"

"Something like that." I said.

"Something like that." I sat behind her while she drove us home. I loved kissing her, talking to her, just being with this girl. I didn't mind watching her drive, either.

FIFTEEN

Hobie

I'd developed a habit of walking out of the house with my blue jean pockets stuffed full of carrots. The cashiers at the grocery store probably thought I had some strange addiction. Sure, I could take apples to the horses instead, but I liked those for myself. I always picked up carrots at the store, hoping maybe I'd eat a vegetable here and there, but sure enough the carrots always found their way into my pockets, and to the horses instead. Who needs carrots anyway? I ate my apple a day. I was doing just fine.

I climbed up onto the fence and sat down, pulling the carrots out and setting them on my lap. Sampson walked right up to me and went straight for the gold. I pushed his nose back and called him out on it.

"Manners, Sammy." He huffed at me and stomped his feet. "Alright, alright, but be polite." I started to hand out the carrots, a game I'd come to enjoy. One a piece, back and forth, taking turns. I was starting to wonder what kind of tricks I could teach them with these carrots. Then I thought to myself that things were going just fine as they were. No sense in making anything difficult. They were old boys, and they probably enjoyed not doing a damn thing. Not to mention, at their age they'd probably well earned a life of stability and ease.

With mouthfuls, Tigua and Sampson munched for a while and I looked out across the stables, just in time to see Ruby jogging up the driveway. That was about the best view on the property. Well, any view with Ruby in it was a good one. But I had really come to appreciate her morning runs. She hated running when I moved here, and made it pretty clear that she would never join me, at least not willingly. Maybe I motivated her, maybe not. I didn't really care what got her running, I just enjoyed watching. Selfish? Yeah, maybe.

She continued along the driveway, around the main house, behind the stables, and stopped down at the water's edge, to sit and rest like she did most mornings.

She pulled the headphones from her ears as I sat down.

"Morning." I rested my arms on my knees and joined her, looking out at heaven. No wonder she stopped here every morning.

"Good morning." She was trying not to let me see the smile plastered across her face, but she wasn't too good at hiding it. "What's on the books for the day, cowboy?"

"Cowboy?" I laughed.

"Well, I'm not supposed to call you the ranch hand because apparently this isn't a ranch. So, what do you prefer then? Lone ranger? Wrangler? Buckaroo? Those all sound ridiculous. Shephard? We don't have any sheep." She turned her head to me, looking surprised. "Oh man. We totally need sheep. How *cute* would that be? Then you really could be the shepherd! Goats, too."

"Let's stick with the horses for now."

"Alright, alright. But for the record, I'd really like to get some sheep." She didn't need to clarify that. With the joy across her face when she mentioned it, it was an idea I would never forget. I was certain that one day, she—we— would have sheep.

"Well, I was just over there having breakfast with the guys," I diverted back to the original conversation, and away from the family planning.

"The guys?" She looked over to the stables. "Tigua and Sampson are the guys?"

"You know. Working on friendships. I've really developed a quality relationship with those two."

"A pocket full of carrots doesn't count, Hobie. That's not friendship, it's bribery."

"So, how do I bribe you, then?"

"You don't have to bribe me." She leaned back and laid across the grass, eyes closed to soak in the sunshine above us. "Though, I wouldn't mind another attempt at dinner."

"That's not really what I had in mind, Ruby." I knew what she was getting at. She wanted me to come back to the house for family dinner again tonight.

"You can't get past it if you don't keep trying. And who knows, maybe if you get comfortable here, we could try something new. Like one of Sam's soccer games. Or a surf competition with Roy." She'd turned to look at me, tugging at the hem of my shirt. I leaned back, laying down next to her in the grass and closing my eyes as I settled into the ground.

Not too long ago, I wouldn't have been able to feel this way. Not only was it nice, being here with her. But I could actually feel the rays of sunshine touch my face. I could feel the grass cushion beneath my shoulders. The breeze sounded like a constant whisper from the surface of the sea. The things that I noticed now, the way I felt, was actually tangible. The darkness from before, that hovered above me and around me like wet cement kept all of those things away. They didn't matter, because none of it could cut through the weight. These days, the weight had it's moments. But more often than not, I felt like my senses were alive again. This moment right here, feeling this way, was something I'd dreamed of for years now: the ability to breathe the world in and just *be*.

I could have stayed right there forever, right here next to her. As much as I didn't yet understand exactly what was happening, or what would happen next, I knew without a doubt that this was the right place to be, and she was the right person to be here with.

"I don't need to try anything tonight. I could probably use a quiet night at the house anyway."

Her fingers brushed across mine in the grass, and before I knew it, I had a grip on her hand, hanging on for dear life. It was like my fingers belonged around hers.

"You're not going to get a quiet night at the house, Hobie. The whole place is going to be a loud mess. And Roy wants to see your blood."

"That's disgusting," I looked at my hand, which had mostly healed. I only kept it wrapped for a little cushion while I worked.

"He's ten. And he's Roy. What do you expect?"

"I know." I pulled her hand up to my chest, brushing my thumb across her knuckles. I was acutely aware of every single move she made, of every movement that brought us closer together or farther apart.

"Well. You're going to have to come back eventually. What if you just stopped running from it all, and just... just walked with me?"

She had a point. Truthfully, I'd have walked anywhere with her, and that was the scariest part. It wasn't the idea of getting settled here in Wrightsville, or on the estate. The scariest part was that no matter what I did, I wanted to do it all with her. It's exactly what I had been avoiding all these years, and I couldn't do it anymore. There was nothing I could do now to keep myself away from her. I was starting to feel human again. And I was drawn to her like a fish to bait. I needed her, no matter the risk.

"I have to get going. I have to shower and get to the cafe." She sat up, and turned to look at me.

"What are you thinking?" I asked, as she held her eyes on me.

"I'm thinking... I can't tell you what I'm thinking." She stood up and put her headphones back into her ears, with a guilty smile across her face.

"It's okay. Don't tell me. I don't have time to go with you anyway."

"Awfully presumptuous of you, assuming that I wanted you to come with me." She raised her eyebrows like she was challenging me.

I stood up to face her, and leaned in to her, nose to nose.

"But you did," I whispered.

She blushed, kissed my cheek, and took off. Loving her was simple.

The rest of my morning finished up pretty fast. I stopped by the cafe to get some lunch, which doubled as an excuse to see her again. Port knew about us at this point, but otherwise no one had mentioned it. Loving her out loud around everyone else was something I'd have to check off the list, but I was feeling brave. I was going out of my way to see her, and I wasn't worried about who else would be there to see it. It was almost as if having friends and family was starting to feel normal. The usual harassment you might get from friends and siblings about a new relationship seemed natural, and I felt like I was getting close enough to everyone here that the harassment might be fitting, entertaining even.

"There he is! The horse whisperer himself." Eddy hollered from the cafe bar.

"Well, I wouldn't go that far." I climbed up onto the only open stool, right in the middle of the rest of them. It almost felt like they were saving it for me. Ruby was leaning across the counter on the other side with the rest of the ladies, feeding their men.

"Oh, please. You're the first person Sampson hasn't tried to kill. You've got something special." Ruby said.

"Mhmm." Penny added, sipping from her mug and tossing her eyes between Ruby and me. I felt myself blush, acutely aware that Penny knew. I wondered what everyone else knew, and what they thought about this crazy new guy and the influence he could have on their perfect baby girl. Honestly, underneath the bravery there was a part of me that still got caught up in wondering why they would encourage Ruby to spend any time with a mess of a man like me, a man with no family, no friends, and shatters a glass the second he hears a loud noise. Old habits die hard. Maybe I'd let that go sooner than later.

"Lunchtime, man." Port leaned forward, looking past Rhett and Eddy to me, down the bar, "what'll it be?"

"I'm alright, thanks. I'll grab something at the house." Port shot me a glare, and I knew he was challenging me; give it a shot. Make friends. Let them walk with me.

Ruby walked up just then and laid a plate in front of me. Scrambled eggs, toast, and some sort of grilled fish.

"Or not." It smelled delicious. "Thank you, Ruby."

"Of course." She went back to the register and helped another customer. I watched her as she walked away, fighting an obscene smile until my eyes crossed Port's. Suddenly I realized that everyone was looking right at me. I choked on my dry throat a bit and reached for my fork and dug in. Penny slid a glass of water over to me, still staring with that sweet smile. She was such a mom. She didn't hide a single thing she felt about anyone in her family. And now she was doing the same with me.

"Thank you." I took a sip and kept my eyes back down at my plate. This got awkward real fast. I put my food down as fast as I could while the rest of them talked, and quietly observed. Standing to leave, I noticed that Ruby was occupied with another customer. So, I nodded to the guys and reached for my wallet to leave cash for the food.

"Put your wallet away, son. She ain't charging you." Rhett huffed. Eddy and Port smiled with their heads down like they were trying to stay out of it, but they didn't add anything further.

"Family eats for free, son." There was a lot packed into such a small sentence, and Eddy knew it. But something told me he didn't talk just to talk. Eddy calling me family made me actually believe it.

"Yes, sir." I hung my head with a smile, and put my wallet away. "Y'all have a good afternoon, then."

"So we'll see you at dinner, Hobie?" Port turned on his stool.

"Uh..." I opened the door and turned to look back at him, not sure of what to say. "Maybe, yeah. Thanks." I left, realizing that something was still holding me back from joining them. For whatever reason, I wasn't ready to go back. Not yet.

I spent the rest of the afternoon in the gardens, adding to the designs for the irrigation system and making a few last minute adjustments. Penny seemed excited about it, and wanted to see my ideas in drawings before we got started. I wanted to make sure that we built a system that not only took care of the gardens as they were, but created potential for growth as well. The family had a lot of plans for this place, and the best thing for me to do was to work like it was my own.

I managed to get back to the house a bit earlier than usual, so I packed a cooler and grabbed a six pack. When I saw the first few cars pull up to the main house for dinner, I made my way down to the marina. I decided that the only real way I was going to avoid dinner was to jump on the boat and get off the island entirely.

Knowing I might need an escape route, I left everything uncovered earlier after a quick trip out to the Erv, which made it quick and easy to head out again. The longer I was around, the more opportunity someone would have to come hunt me down and make sure that I went to dinner.

Relief about knocked me over when I looked up the hill, and saw her walking toward me. If I could have one view for the rest of my life, that would be it. Ruby had those dark blue jeans on, the ones that were tight in all the right places. Her usual top, a simple, black, sleeveless thing that fell off her shoulders just right. She had a sweatshirt draped over her arm and a bag in her hand. Her long hair was braided down to the side, with that flowery headband I liked so much. It was dressed up for her, similar to what she usually wore to the cafe, and it was perfect. I didn't say a word. I just let her come on down to me, watching each step, and every loose hair blow around her face in the breeze.

"Where are *you* going?" I asked, a bit sarcastically, hoping like hell that she wasn't about to leave me to go to that dinner.

"Wherever you're taking me." She said, climbing onto the boat. She dropped her bag and put on her sweatshirt, and began to help me untie from the dock; like this was the plan all along and as if we'd done this a thousand times before. "You can't run from it forever, Hobie."

"I know. But tonight's not the night."

"So. What's tonight then?" She asked with a suspicious smile.

"Tonight is... quiet. I need some quiet time, some time with you. I was going to head out until I couldn't see the island anymore. Maybe just sit there for a while. Settle my head down, you know." I keyed the engine, and leaned back against the seat.

She climbed into the chair behind me, and I pulled out of the marina without a thought. I was creating habits here. I was doing something that I'd done enough times that it didn't take any thought. I could do this with my eyes closed. The familiarity was nice. I wasn't sure if I'd ever get used to things like that again. Getting out after a day at work, me and her. This was what I'd waited for; the possibility that life was about more than surviving. That was an idea I had been desperate to believe in for years. For the first time, it occured to me that I couldn't walk away. I'd leave too much behind.

"Will you tell me what you're thinking?" She asked, drawing her fingers over my hand, back and forth.

I was hesitant to let her know how deep in thought I really was, but if she was going to know me, if she was going to choose me, I figured maybe I should go ahead and keep being honest with her about it all. After all, she was still sticking around.

"Have you ever felt like... none of it really mattered? Like maybe, tomorrow wasn't really worth fighting for?" I didn't look her in the eyes when I said that. She was still sitting behind me, but her fingers reached for a tighter grip on my hands, and I knew then that she felt the weight of what I was asking.

"Is that how you feel?" She asked.

"No." A laugh escaped, mixed with a deep breath. "Not at all, quite the opposite actually. Right now is the first time in a while that I've... I don't remember the last time I felt like that. Well, I do remember, but it's been a bit... not since I got here."

"So that's how you felt before?"

I caught my breath again, desperate for the bravery I knew this conversation would take, and turned around to face her. This was something I needed her to know, and I wanted to see her face when I told her. I needed her to know the most honest parts of me, the years of my life that made me who I am, that made me the guy she knew and loved. And I wanted her to truly understand how far I'd come.

"Ruby, did Port tell you that I didn't have a job when I applied for this one?"

"No. Port didn't tell me anything about you. Honestly, he just said he'd finally found some help."

"So... the day Port called, I wasn't exactly... at my best. It was just one of those days where I was feeling the weight of it all. Like it all caught up with me. Being so alone... I was really feeling it, you know? I realized that I had gone at least a week without looking another person in the eye. Like nine or ten days, without anyone acknowledging me at all. Without anyone saying a single word to me. I realized that no one noticed me. So, then I realized that no one would notice if I was gone, either. Being gone actually started to sound better than being around, but alone."

I turned in time to see her process what I'd said, and watched as the emotion hit her face, and her eyes fell. "I'd notice." She whispered.

"That's the thing though. I have this joy now. I have a reason to wake up tomorrow, and it's not just you. It's what you—and your family—have given to me, and what this place has taught me. I didn't know you then. I didn't have anyone. It wasn't like it is here. I was literally, completely alone, and I didn't want to be alone anymore. I didn't want to *be* anymore, Ruby."

She wiped a tear from her cheek. I knew she understood what I was getting at. But I still had to say it. I had to lay everything out.

"Everyone I'd ever loved had died, and even more had been hurt because of me... and that was as good as it was going to get. So I'd decided that... not *being* anymore... It seemed exciting. You know, it seemed like more than... it seemed like the next logical thing to do, a goal I could accomplish"

"But here you are." She said through another tear.

"Because Port called. Ruby, it was... honestly it was down to the minute. I had the lid off of a full bottle of pills, and a full fifth of whiskey. I was ready, but then Port called. He asked how I was doing, and said he had a job for me and a place to live. Honestly, Ruby, that's all it took, right then. All it took to get my mind off things was the idea of having someone to check in with, having something to do with my hands again."

She climbed up onto her knees on the seat and leaned her chest against mine, with her hands on my shoulders. "You didn't want to *be*."

"But Ruby. You make me feel like I can. Like I can exist. Like I *do* exist."

"You more than exist to me, Hobie. I can't imagine a world without you in it. We made plans. We have ideas for the future, and you're in them. This place, before you got here, it doesn't make sense anymore." She leaned her forehead against mine. "Promise me you understand that. Promise me you get it, how much you matter to me, Hobie. How much I—"

"I love you, Ruby."

"I love you too, Hobie. Promise me you know that." She pulled her face away enough to look back into my eyes, and it killed me to see her tears falling.

"I know. I do." She kissed me quickly, but it was the way she hugged me that told me what I needed to know. It was like she couldn't get around me fast enough. She pulled her arms so tight around my neck, and crossed her feet behind my back like her life depended on it. She understood. Now I could say that she knew the deepest, darkest parts of me and she was still choosing me.

"I just needed you to know that. I needed to tell you, because I want you to know everything. I don't want to keep things from you. I love you. So much." I whispered into her hair as she clung to me. As bad as things were before, as low as I'd fallen... here she was, loving me anyway. I didn't think anyone could, or would, ever again.

I knew what that was like, unconditional love. My mom was incredible. My brother was my best friend. But this is the first time since losing them, and everyone else, that the possibility of unconditional love felt stronger than the risk of loss. It was still my greatest fear, that something could happen to her, or that she would decide to walk away. But for right now, loving her felt better. I felt like a boat that couldn't drop an anchor. I was getting tossed back and forth in the waves, at night and in a storm. But I finally got the anchor down, and even though I was still getting tossed in the waves, I wasn't getting tossed quite so far.

We laid on the deck of the boat for a while, enjoying the silence and the sway of the tide until I felt like I needed to get us home.

"You awake?" I asked quietly.

"Yeah."

"I bet dinner's over."

"Probably. Will you take me home, Hobie?"

"Yes, ma'am." I kissed her with a smile.

I knew that boat could go, but I didn't know the feeling of driving it that fast, until now. It was fun, sure. Maybe another day I'd have to do that again so that I could really take the time to enjoy it. Something about an engine that loud, and that kind of wind. It was a freedom I hadn't known before.

Not right then, though. At that moment, I was more focused on getting that girl home. We needed to get off that boat, and up the hill. I docked us and tied the boat to the cleats faster than I should have, probably not doing the best job. I only managed one good knot before I found myself chasing her up the hill and up the stairs, onto her back porch. She'd stumbled crossing the deck and getting to the door, which I noticed she'd kept unlocked.

I caught up with her at the door, and turned her shoulders to face me before she even had the chance to open it.

"Ruby. We don't have to—" She hooked a few fingers into my shirt collar, and pulled us close.

"Yes." She interrupted, before a quick kiss. "Yes we do." Before I knew it she was pulling me over the threshold, and slammed the door.

By the time we'd reached the top of the stairs, face to face was the only place I ever wanted to be again. I wanted to breathe the same air as Ruby for the rest of time.

"Please stay with me tonight." She begged, keeping her mouth close to mine.

The streetlights jumped through the blinds, and a few rays of their light landed directly on her bed. Her eyes glistened in those rays, her perfect shade of blue, when I laid her down. In the darkness, with nothing but the street lights shining in, those blue eyes were begging me for everything else. I ran my thumb across the blush of her cheeks, noticing that the nerves she had before were gone. Her hesitations and her wonder. They had all been traded for a powerful confidence and safety.

She smelled like a mixture of the salty sea and some kind of rosey freshness. It was the same scent I'd noticed when I first walked into the cottage, the same scent I'd smelled all last night before falling asleep. Even though she'd moved out of the guest house and taken her things with her, she was still there. That scent was all I had for a while. I had her in the back of my mind all along, and didn't even know it. That scent smelled like home.

"This is the only place I ever want to be again. Right here with you." She said.

"You want to keep me here?" I joked.

"No," She laughed, gripping my shirt and tugging me even closer. "Here."

I found myself getting tossed between her innocence, and the way she seemed to need me at the same time. Something, I wasn't sure what exactly, but something about being there with her already felt like the groundwork of forever. Neither one of us second guessed what we were doing. Now that we had been together, being apart was what felt wrong. Nothing about her felt new or unknown, she just felt like mine. So I made it clear to her, earth-shatteringly clear, that we were going to spend the rest of time together.

Laying there with her felt permanent. I started to wonder what I had missed by running away from her all this time.

"I'm sorry Ruby. I'm sorry I wasted any time with you." She kissed my hands. I kissed her shoulder, settling down on the pillow behind her.

"We're here now. That's all that matters."

"You're never allowed to leave." I kissed the back of her head.

"It's my house." she laughed. "I think you're going to be spending a lot more time here though."

"What's wrong with my place?"

"Way too close." She rolled over, and snuggled back into me, her nose to mine. "I plan on spending entirely too much time with you, and I'd prefer we be as far away from my family as possible."

"Oh really?" I smiled.

"Mhmm. Problem?"

"No, ma'am. Not one bit."

I fell into that deep train of thought again. What took so long? Why couldn't I have found her sooner? Why couldn't I have had her with me before? You're supposed to have a hand to hold through the hard stuff. You're supposed to have someone to call home, when the world gets tough. Why did I have to do all of that alone?

Just as I realized what I was committing my heart to—that I was going to make certain for the rest of time that neither one of us would have to do anything alone again—I suddenly felt devastated as I realized that I could have lost all of this. I could have done something to ruin what was possible here, what was waiting for me. I could have walked away from her, before I even knew her. As I was falling asleep, I realized that I was living a miracle.

When I opened my eyes again, I was surprised that she was still wrapped up in my arms, in the very same place she had been before. The sunlight poured through the window, and I could hear the morning mix of the boats down at the marina pulling out for the day, and the noise next door at the cafe. I slowly opened my eyes to the first morning I could remember that didn't feel like I *had* to face another day. Instead, I felt lucky that I got to take one more look at this beautiful woman in my arms. I was full of joy, and thankful for her. Feeling like she was grace, given to me. She was the hope, and the home, I'd been looking for.

SIXTEEN

Ruby

"Hobie." I whispered quietly. I didn't want to wake him.

"Mhmmm" he mumbled, his scruff brushing against the back of my neck.

"I want to take you somewhere this morning."

"Does it involve food?"

I laughed. "No. But we can stop for breakfast on the way. I know a place."

"Why don't we start with the stables? If we get the horses taken care of this morning, I can spend most of the day with you. Unless of course you're trying to get rid of me."

I rolled over to face him. "Not a chance." Part of me was amazed that he was still here this morning. The man who had run away every chance he had so far, had stayed all night, again. The one who always had a reason to walk away. The one who wouldn't spend time with the family. The one who resembled 'back and forth' better than anyone I knew. Here he was, showing signs of consistency.

"You stayed," I continued. "I'm surprised, I thought maybe yesterday was a fluke."

"Me too." He said. Neither one of us had yet to move, and honestly, I was afraid to, like if I broke this moment we might never get it back.

"I'm kind of afraid, that if we get up and leave, that you won't make it back here to me again."

He reached his hand across my cheek, brushing my forehead and through my hair.

"I only ever wanted to keep my distance to keep you safe... to keep myself from getting attached, and getting hurt." He said. "It's different now. I'm scared to death, Ruby. I'm so afraid of losing you, but I'm also afraid of not being with you at all. I can't. I really don't think I could do it."

"Then don't." I said. "Just stay." I leaned in, my forehead to his. "Let's just figure it out, together. Okay? Day at a time. It's been working well so far."

"Okay, but I was also thinking. What if you and I snuck away for a weekend? Just the two of us. Away from everyone here. Away from the estate. What if we just got away for a night or two?"

"When can we leave?" I smiled. I would have left right that second if he'd wanted to.

He kissed my forehead and took a deep breath. "I'll figure something out. First, tell me about this breakfast." He really had mastered the art of changing the subject.

I sat up and jumped out of bed, racing across the room. He tossed the covers and chased me straight into the shower, inches behind me the whole way. Breakfast could wait.

We walked along the park on South Channel, and over the bridge toward the island. At the top of the bridge, looking south over the water, I stopped and stared. Hobie stood behind me, and around me, resting his chin on my shoulder.

"This is my second favorite place on the island." I said.

He kissed my neck. "Tell me why you love it so much."

I took in the sailboats that were mooring below. There were usually more, but this morning it was quiet.

"It's interesting to me, how all four of them seem so similar. The body, the design, the sails. The direction they all face. It's like they're a fleet, all traveling and anchored here together."

"Makes a nice view." He added, drawing his fingertips over the top of my hand.

"But think about how different they really are. It's incredible."

"What do you mean?"

"Well. The boats. They all look pretty much the same, and they're all docked here in the same water right now. But, there's no telling where they've been. We have no idea who's driving, or who's living on those boats. We don't know where

210

they're going next or where they came from last, but you can still stand here and soak in the beauty of it. You can stare at that sailboat, and admire everything about it, all without knowing a single thing. It's just perspective."

"I'm glad you see things that way. I wonder what I'd be missing out on if you couldn't have looked at me that way."

"That's just it. You can stand here, far away, and admire it all. But until you get up close, and step onto that boat, you won't see where the sails have been worn down from storms. Where the deck has been scratched. You won't know until you go and ask where the captain has been, or where he wants to go. You know, every time the winds change, he has to change his workload. He has to redirect, maybe make a new plan."

I didn't want to stand here and cry. I wanted to show him the joy of it and the beauty of this place that I called home, but what hit me was the weight of it; the emotional gravity of the land and the sea, and the constant conflict between the two. How one wouldn't exist without the other.

"Hobie," I turned around to face him. "All those rips and tears, all the scratches, the notches in the wood... the sails might be torn, but they've seen the most beautiful pieces of the world. If they had never taken the chance and gone out there, and risked getting torn, they wouldn't have gotten to sail through those places. They wouldn't be able to tell us the stories, or bring a piece of the world back here to the island, for the rest of us."

"I'm really torn up. Really scratched." He hung his head. I reached to lift his chin back up.

"And look at you! You've brought the most incredible pieces of the world with you. Your life, your experience. It's been tough, but incredible. And it brought you here to me. I'd rather have the sailboats here, torn and scratched and worn, because look how beautiful they make this place. What would looking out to the ocean be if you didn't see the sails?"

"You've really thought about this." He said.

"No, Hobie. I've wondered. For years, I've wondered about these things, and wondered what was missing. I've sat here for years and wondered why everything seemed almost perfect, but not quite. I've wondered what was left out there, all while never wanting to leave here to find it. And then you came here."

"I came here. So, now what do you think?"

"I think that I understand now why the sails get torn, and the decks get scratched. I know now why the anchors rust. It's because of everything it took for them to get here, still on top of the water. Boats are only perfect until they get into the ocean. The ocean might damage them, but the ocean is where they're supposed to be. It's what they were created for."

"I wish it hadn't taken so long to find you," he whispered.

"We just had to get our sails torn up a bit first. A perfect boat on a showroom floor doesn't have a story to tell." I answered. "Come on. I want to show you my actual favorite place."

"Have you come here?" I asked as we walked through the gates.

"Only to the beach. I like walking in the sand."

I took his hand and led him out to the end of the pier.

I thought through all of this for years, but I never really took the time to explain it to anyone. Or, maybe I just never had the chance. "You know, when I'm in the water, I can feel the gravity. It's like when you're sitting in the ocean, you become fully aware of the weight of the world as the swell is pulling you in. But it depends on you. Because you can sit there, floating on top of the ocean, and you can surf, and you can swim, and it feels like the ocean is the safest place to be. I've always felt like the ocean was... was—"

"Like grace?" He cut me off with my very own thought. He'd finally put words to the part I'd stumbled over. The part that I couldn't quite define. He continued. "The wave can be really heavy, and feel like it's going to drown you forever. But if you can get your head up just enough, you could ride that same wave all the way into shore. It can kill you, or it can bring you home."

"It all depends on how you look at it." He was changing. The Hobie that moved here would have only seen the drowning. He never would have given the ride a chance. I couldn't believe what I was hearing. He had hope. "And then, the ocean will wait right here for you to come back. Because no matter what you're carrying, no matter how heavy you feel, you can come back here

213

and let it go. It's like the ocean was never trying to drown me in the first place, and I had it all wrong."

"Exactly." I looked up to him, noticing the redness, and swelling in his eyes.

"I guess, it's just that for so long, I felt like I was drowning. The same tide, the same wave that everyone else felt like they were surfing, was the same thing that was killing me. Drowning me over and over again."

We reached the end of the pier and leaned on the railing over the edge. I knew exactly how to answer him.

"That's why I like coming up here." I said. "When you're down there, you can't see this. You can't see how great it is, how powerful. This ocean, it could flood this island in a second—but it doesn't. The tide only comes so far. This thing that is so great, and so powerful, it skirts up against the coast so carefully. It has the power to end the world, but it has the beauty and the softness to create this—a view like this. That's the kind of thing that makes me think that this is heaven. Right here. In the balance between everything the world is capable of is where I feel the most peace."

"I worry sometimes though. I worry that no matter how good I get at surfing, I could still drown." He challenged me. And he had a point.

"Rogue waves," I thought. "I guess, if something comes and knocks you down, we just have to remember to change your view. The water isn't so heavy when you're up on the pier."

"This is what I needed." He looked out over to the north side of the pier. "Look, it's Roy."

It was. Roy, and Sam, and a whole bunch of their friends. A usual sight, even for a weekday morning.

"I'm going to go out on a limb here and assume that Penny thinks they're in school." I laughed. I couldn't blame them, since I had done the same thing pretty regularly when I was younger. The boys would do anything they could to get into the water, and once I was old enough, I got rolled up into it all. "Not that Port would have any ground to stand on, yelling at them for it. He pulled the same stunt more times than I could count. He's the one that taught me how to get away with it." I leaned my elbows on the edge of the pier, watching the boys in their element.

There was something so full circle about it.

My parents met here. Raised us here, taught us how to live on the water, and then dealt with the blowback everytime we got in trouble for it. Now here we were watching Port's kids doing the exact same thing, and I was to them what my Aunt Nori wanted to be for us. A piece of what I missed out on, was happening right here in front of me. There's the grace.

"Wait a second." Hobie pushed from his elbows to his hands, leaning farther over the pier, intently focused on the boys. "He didn't come back."

"Who?" I asked, trying to catch up.

"Right there. That white board. Where'd he go?" He was pointing out to the group, just as we saw the boys start to toss around. Serenity turned to commotion below us and I started to grasp what was happening about the same time as all of the kids. One of them hadn't come back up. There was a board with no one on it.

Before I knew it, Hobie had kicked off his shoes and pulled off his sweatshirt. He climbed up onto the railing of the pier as the boys started to yell for help.

"Hobie, stop. Don't!" He was gone before I could finish. When he resurfaced, I caught my breath. As he raced toward the boys, I ran down the pier and down the stairs into the sand, as fast as I could, though it wouldn't ever have felt fast enough. Keegan, one of the boys' friends had paddled in and ran straight into me, ankle deep in the water.

"Ruby! Ruby, get help!" His words caught up to his breaths, and he grabbed onto my hands like his own life depended on it.

"I know, buddy. Come here." I pulled the phone to my ear, and Keegan to my side. As usual, the response happened faster than you'd think was possible. The first truck from ocean rescue pulled right in front of us, skidding to a stop in the sand. The driver jumped out, and ran to the water. A few on four wheelers, another one of the trucks, and the nearest guards on foot, all filed in one by one. It was the oddest combination of chaos and routine, unexpected but rehearsed, tragic yet simple.

Keegan clung to me, and Tyler came out of the water and joined us on my other side. I hugged them close, and could feel their fear seep through from their skin to mine. I would have taken all of it, if I could. I felt Keegan's heartbeat race. Tyler turned his head into my shoulder, just trying to look away. There was nothing I could do to help in the water. All I could do was keep the boys with me, and keep them safe while everyone else took care of the kids in the water. This was a hell of a reminder, they were just kids; just boys. When they're out playing, at school, or around the house, they seem so grown sometimes... but in a moment of fear, where everything was wrong, and the boys were in danger, I remembered. They were just boys.

We watched as countless swimmers from ocean rescue ran into the water. Hobie and the rest of the boys had been diving and surfacing over and over. A jet ski pulled up from behind the pier right as Hobie surfaced again with the boy tossed over his shoulder. Hobie reached up to a handle on the tail of the ski, and held on as they pulled into shore.

Hobie and the guard pulled the boy up and onto the sand as Sam, Roy, and the rest of their friends paddled in behind them.

"Boys!" I waved. "Boys, come here!" They dropped their boards on the sand and ran past the crowd to me. "Roy, who is that?" I asked as I watched the guards start chest compressions. I tried to get the kids to face me, rather than watch what was happening.

"It's Reed. I don't know what happened. He paddled into one and rolled off, and he never came back up. Reed Sollerton." The Sollertons had lived just over the bridge on the main land for years. Jack Sollerton was a teacher at the high school. Minutes had gone by now, and I heard yelling come from the crowd.

When I looked back to them, Hobie stood up and wiped his face as his head fell back. The guys on the outside of the crowd, mostly ocean rescue guys that we knew, were all catching their breath, visibly relieved. I watched as a few of them tossed their hats on the ground and caught their breath. One collapsed down with his arms around his knees. He'd been the last one with his hands on the boy. The captain walked over to him and kneeled behind him, hand on his shoulder. After a minute, the two stood up, and the captain hugged him briefly before shaking his hand and patting him on the back.

"Ruby." I heard softly behind me.

"Hey Dad." Relief seeped through me when he rested his arm around my shoulders, another around Sam and Roy. Uncle Eddy took a few slow steps in front of me, stopping just shy of the crowd with his hands on his hips. He reached up to adjust his cap, a telltale sign that he was remembering rescues and losses of his own. One in particular went south right here at this pier. He lost a little boy a long time ago in one of his first few summers with the squad. If you caught him on a good day, he'd tell you just a little bit about it. Legend has it though, that his captain and Aunt Nori are the only other two that know the whole story.

Hobie emerged from the crowd, and he walked toward us until Sam and Roy met him in the middle. I smiled when they clung to him. For a moment, I hoped that Hobie felt it too. I wanted him to feel in the depths of his soul how much those boys needed him then. In the scariest experience of their lives, they ran to *him*. In a moment where they needed help, *he* was there—and I needed him to feel that.

Hobie dropped to his knees and wrapped his arms around the boys as they hugged him. He looked past their shoulders to me and almost smiled. I nodded, trying to keep my hands around the rest of them. I couldn't believe what had just happened. We'd gone from laughing at the boys skipping school, to thanking God that they were all okay.

Captain Wheaton walked over to us all huddled in the sand.

"I'm sorry, Cap." Tyler cried. "I'm so sorry." Wheat kneeled in front of Tyler and grabbed his shoulders.

"You did the right thing son. You got help as fast as you could. And he's alright, see?" They all turned to look back to Reed. "You boys did a fine job. I'm proud of you."

"We're all going to have a little chat about skipping school, so that I can tell your parents I handled it. But as far as this goes, you boys did everything you should have done, you did good." Cap was always good with the kids, but he had an extra special ability to encourage and inspire them in the hardest of times. If you were lucky, you'd only have to hear about it, but some kids had the unfortunate experience of getting one of Cap's speeches face to face.

"We're just so glad you are all okay," I added.

The guard who had done the chest compressions joined us then. "Hey fellas, have any of you ever seen your friend have a seizure?"

A few of them looked confused, but Roy answered. "Yes sir. There's a medicine he has to take every morning. I've seen his dad bring it to him at school when he's forgotten before." The guard nodded and looked to Captain Wheaton. "Sometimes he takes one before dinner, too."

"That's right," Hobie added. "His dad came to dinner one night, and said he'd forgotten to take his medicine. Said it couldn't wait."

"Sir, it's looking like he may be postictal." Wheaton seemed to know exactly what the guard was talking about. "Heck of a bite through his tongue, got the bleeding under control though. Best we can assume for the time being. We're going to get him over to Regional now, and Noah is going to head over to the school to get his dad."

"Good job, man." They shook hands. "I'll see you back at headquarters. I'll get everything set up for a debrief."

Cap turned back to Hobie. "And you, sir. Well normally I'd point out that jumping off the pier is illegal. But in this case, I'd rather say that I am mighty glad you were there. Thank you." Hobie nodded, with a humble handshake.

"Come on boys." Eddy said. "Grab your boards. Time to go."

"What does postal mean?" Sam asked.

"Postictal." Eddy corrected. "It's kind of like... how someone is feeling after a seizure."

"Did that happen because he swallowed water? He was drowning?" Tyler asked.

"No, if he had a seizure, then I'd bet that's probably what caused him to go under in the first place. Most likely, seizure started, and he never came back up." Eddy explained gently. There was only so much you could explain to a ten year old.

"You know guys, what happened today was scary—and it's okay if you're scared, you know. It scared me too." Dad started. The boys all looked to each other, and you could almost tell that they were all a bit afraid to speak up. "Part of being a man is being able to tell someone when you're having a hard time, and then being there for your friends when they're having a hard time too. So if you're not feeling good about all this, it's okay. We can talk about it."

Roy and Sam hugged onto Hobie and me, while the rest of them led the way in with Dad and Eddy. The way Hobie was with the boys was amazing; something I'd only expect from a parent. I hated that this had happened this morning, but it felt like it might have been the first time that Hobie got to see his own true colors and the personality he keeps buried so deep inside. Because deep down, there's a man who can handle anything, and then turn around to help others get through it too. I just don't think he realized that.

"Come on, boys. Let's go home." I said. Hobie, Roy, Sam, and I started walking back to the estate, while Dad and Eddy took the rest of the kids in the truck. If I knew my dad, he'd be gone for a while making sure each kid got settled at home with their parents. The boys seemed as brave as grown men after an incident like that, but they were still just ten years old. I was proud of them, but also worried.

As I walked into the kitchen, two lunch plates had already been set out for the boys. News traveled fast. Penny and Port must have known we were coming, because by the time the boys sat down to take a bite, their parents were sitting there with them, and the incident report started over the radio.

"Well, boys." Penny said, stirring a fresh pitcher of tea. "Seems you had an interesting morning."

"Yeah. Nothing too crazy." I laughed, and kissed the boys heads before I stepped away to pour a cup of coffee. Hobie joined me, and leaned onto his elbows on the counter.

"I take it you're going to start with telling your parents how sorry you are that you skipped school?" Hobie asked.

"Yes, sir." Sam answered.

"I'd really, really, love it if y'all didn't scare me like that again, okay?" Hobie reached over the island and ruffled Roy's hair.

"You boys keep us on our toes, that's for sure." Penny said. "I tell you what. I'm inclined to ground y'all until the end of time for skipping school, again, but Captain Wheaton called and told us that you all helped to save that boy's life. So I think this time, you're going to owe Hobie a week's worth of work in the stables, and I'll call it even."

Port chimed in. "You know boys, I spoke with Uncle Buckley this morning. He invited us all out for a vacation." Penny winked and the boys' faces lit up with the joy they were lacking. Uncle Buckley was Nori's best friend from college. He usually came to visit around the holidays each year. And every few years we'd all fly out to visit him.

"So if you want to go out to California to see him, I'd suggest you keep your tails out of trouble for a while." Port added, stealing a slice of apple from Sam's plate.

"Yes, sir." They replied solemnly.

"Is that alright with you, Hobie? Can they help with the stables?" Penny asked.

"Works for me. Actually, that's good timing. I was going to ask you, Port, if I could uh..." Hobie looked back at me with a smile across his face. "I was wondering if I could take a few days off. I was thinking about heading out of town for a few days. Long weekend or something."

"Sure thing, man. I think Sam and Roy here can carry your workload for a few days. Especially if that's how they're avoiding being grounded." Port slapped the boys on the shoulders. "Where are you headed?" He asked.

"Savannah, I think." Hobie looked back to me, "If that's alright with you."

I smiled and agreed. "Yeah, I think we could use a few days away."

"We?" Port asked, looking back and forth between us.

"Ohhhhh..." the boys mocked sing-songy until Penny smacked the back of their heads.

I wasn't quite sure exactly what to say. Penny smiled a knowing grin as she poured everyone a fresh glass of tea.

I took a sip and set it back down on the table, while the boys giggled.

"You know what, I've gotta cafe..." I stuttered, standing from my chair, trying to shake the sudden jitters from my hands. "Run to the cafe. I mean. Got to get to work. See y'all." I stepped out of the kitchen door and walked away. I wasn't about to have an awkward 'who's dating who' conversation with my brother. He was just going to have to accept it and move right along. I heard the screen door open again behind me, and Hobie ran to catch up with me, scooping me up by the waist and swinging me around him. I kissed him, laughing.

"That wasn't subtle." I joked.

"I'm done being subtle, Ruby Dixon. You're mine, and I'm going to make sure everyone knows it."

SEVENTEEN

Ruby

The drive down to Savannah gave us a few hours to brainstorm all the fun things we could get into. Granted, I spent quite a bit of that time asleep across the bench seat. We had great intentions for our weekend away, places to eat, things to see. We even locked our phones in the truck, disconnecting from the world—and more importantly, my overwhelming family.

However, after dinner the first night at Planter's Tavern, where I was admittedly a bit overserved, and the subsequent carriage ride through town back to our room, we never did get to the rest of the things on our list. We'd gotten a room for the weekend at The Galloway, a bed and breakfast in Historic Downtown Savannah, and we made good use of it.

The next day went about the same way. We spent most of the time alone in our room, taking a few walks for meals. Turns out a day full of *getting to know each other* will make a girl pretty ravenous. Thankfully, a burger joint a block away took care of that. Twice.

After a coffee at a local place the next morning, we started for home. For the first hour or so, we just coasted along with the radio. I drew my attention back in when Hobie reached over and grabbed my hand.

"I know things with us got off to a... slow start." He seemed nervous. "But I guess, everything's been so good this weekend. I'm kind of just wondering if we—"

I reached up and put my finger over his mouth. "I'm going to stop you right there." I said. "I was yours the day I met you, Hobie. So yes, this is how it's going to be from now on." I reached back to his hand. "Now take me home."

He smiled, and kissed the top of my hand before resting our arms on the center console. I kicked my feet up onto the dashboard and barely made it another few minutes before I fell asleep.

Our weekend away wasn't exactly restful, but for the first time away from the estate, Hobie and I got to spend time with each other that didn't revolve around the work to be done or family around us. For a quick weekend, we just got to be Hobie and Ruby, and I got to drown myself in the excitement of new love.

The bumps of the gravel driveway on the estate woke me up.

"Morning, sleepyhead." Hobie said.

"Your fault." I yawned.

"Proudly." He said, pulling into Cottage Row.

As he parked outside my house, he walked around and opened the door for me.

"Gentleman." I kissed him. "I've got to shower and get to the cafe. I'll see you later?"

"Absolutely." He kissed my cheek and slapped my backside as I walked to my front porch. I liked the way he played with me. It had taken a while, but this steady, monotonous, sad man who arrived on the estate a few months ago was now this open book. He was happy, and goofed around. I knew it wasn't just me that did that for him. It was everything. The property, my family, the town. We had everything here that he would ever need to understand what a home should feel like. Plus, he had me.

I spent a long time thinking this place was perfect just the way it was. Now that Hobie was here, now that he was mine, I realized that having it all was an illusion. Really, I just never knew what I was missing.

The come and go of the cafe was just enough of a hum to keep me occupied. Not that I needed a reason to take my mind off Hobie, but it sure did make the day go by a bit faster, keeping my hands busy. I almost got away with it too, but like clockwork, mom and Penny walked through the door, and about jumped onto their seats at the bar. They never said a word, just stared, chins resting in their hands like they were waiting, less than patiently.

"What?" I huffed.

"Oh come on." Penny said. "You go away with Hobie for three days, come back smiling like the sun, and think you aren't going to tell us all about it?"

"So you brought my mom to a conversation where you were hoping to hear about my sex life?" I joked as I walked across the cafe, turning the sign to *closed* and locking the door.

"Okay, first of all, no. Let's just call it love life. I don't particularly want the details of your sex life." Mom answered.

"Speak for yourself." Penny added. "I do."

"Alright mom. I'll sum it up for you. He's incredible, a perfect gentleman. We had a lovely trip, and I am completely, totally, one hundred percent in love with that man." I felt as cheesy as a Hallmark movie, with my eyelashes fluttering as I professed my love for the handsome prince.

Mom smiled with a sigh. "Oh I figured as much... but that's also good to hear."

"Well close your ears or hit the road, because I'm not finished." Penny said, patting her hand on the bar top, rushing me for details. Mom polished off her drink and winked.

"I love you girls. I'll see you later." She unlatched the door and saw herself out, leaving us to get to the nitty gritty.

"Okay look." Penny started. "He smiles at you like you actually created the sun. He's got the eyes of a supermodel, arms like bowling balls, and is as smart as he is handsome. So, don't even try to go with 'it was fine'." She made air quotes with her fingers. "He rocked your world, didn't he?" She looked like she was in the front row of her favorite concert, waiting for the first chord.

"Well. If you must know, I don't particularly have anyone to... compare to. So."

"Okay, well I knew that too." Penny said.

"It was perfect." I fell apart, suddenly wanting to tell her everything. "He's perfect. It's easy. Everything with him feels like we've been together for years. It just seems right."

"Well good. That's how it should be." She answered.

"Penny, he was so dark when he got here. So, hopeless. He seemed like a robot. Just here to eat, work, and go to bed. But now..." I searched for the words.

"It's like he saw the light?"

"No, it's like he found the light, in himself." I said. "He has joy—serious joy. Not just for me, but for his work. For this island. For the boys, and for the estate. It's like he belongs here, and he finally knows it."

Routine came back to me over the next few days. Stables first, cafe by lunch time. Surf lessons in the evening. I watched from the back porch of the cafe as life on the estate hustled like usual. In the past few months, Hobie had established a pretty busy routine. Between the gardens, the horses, mowing, house repairs, and whatever else was waiting to be done, Port and Hobie were always getting into something. Not to mention the traffic increase down at the marina. Port had filled the empty slips over the past month and had newer and larger boats renting slips for higher fees. Uncle Eddy was working with him to clear the rest of the last dock for ocean rescue. They'd housed at least one boat here at our marina ever since Eddy was a kid, but last month they came to Port asking if they could move into a few more slips. Obviously that was a quick yes. It was nice to see the local operations of the town growing while the estate grew too.

Whenever Port decided they needed a break, we'd see him, usually with Hobie, head for the boats. Within an hour or so they'd come back, returning with an impressive sized catch for dinner that night. The two of them got pretty close, and I was enjoying it. It felt good, to love a man and know my family loved him too.

For the first time in a while Mondays had become my favorite day of the week. Monday mornings always served as a reminder that this was how things were going to be from now on, and all the little details were what really made it perfect.

I stepped back inside, startled to find Mom, Penny, and Aunt Allison watching me.

"God, y'all can be creepy sometimes." I hissed, joining Penny at the bar.

"You love that boy something fierce." Aunt Allison couldn't get enough. Somehow or another, me having someone to love made all of her dreams come true.

"I do." I sipped on my coffee, and couldn't knock the smile off my face.

"I think we've known it a whole lot longer than you have." Penny joked. "You guys couldn't just go with it from the very beginning?"

"Ehh. It's all working out now."

"Speaking of, Port and I were hoping y'all would be up for a double date. What do you say? Dinner at Dockside? Ice cream at Flav's?"

"Sounds like a date." I said, shooing off whistles from the old ladies, and running off to the register as a crowd came in. Saved by the tourists.

The morning turned into the afternoon and Penny and I locked up the cafe. The boys stopped in when they got off the bus, helping us finish up mopping the floors. I quizzed Sam on his multiplication and division. He mastered his twelve times-tables and was super proud of it. Roy got good enough grades, but didn't care. He only did enough schoolwork to keep himself eligible for surf competitions. Sam was always looking for the next thing to study.

"Alright, so. I think it's past time I start bringing a dish to dinner." Hobie and I had spent the past hour dancing in the living room of the guest house, sharing silly stories, and well... a fair amount of making out in the kitchen.

"I have an idea." I said, scrolling on my phone. "How about we make something together; we can just bring one big dish instead of two smaller ones. I found a recipe on Pinterest I wanted to try."

"You mean we should bring a couple's dish to dinner? We ought to just get married right now." I shot him a look. The kind that said 'ha ha very funny' even though, truthfully, I was hoping marriage would be on the table one day.

Hobie walked over with two glasses. "That's potent." I noted the alcohol that I could smell from feet away.

"Sorry, I might have been a little heavy handed. It's your favorite." I took a sip and smiled. He liked blackberry brandy, and I liked sweet tea. We'd combined the two during our weekend in Savannah, and I had a new favorite drink.

"Here it is!" I turned my phone to him. "Lemon Garlic Tossed Broccoli."

"Sounds healthy. The boys are going to hate it." He opened the refrigerator and pulled out a few heads of broccoli that we'd gotten from the market that morning. I followed the recipe to make the sauce, diced it all up, dancing around each other in the kitchen while *A Walk To Remember* played on the television in the living room. He made fun of me now and then when he'd look over and see me reciting the words along with the movie.

The noise started to pick up outside as everyone started to show up for dinner. We were ready to go, but I told Hobie we couldn't leave until the movie ended. When it did, I got up from the couch to start getting ready to head over to the house, and Hobie sat back down, noticeably intrigued; maybe confused.

"Wait a second." Hobie said, sprawled out across the couch, still looking irritated as he stared at the television. "All that. All that mess. Fighting with his friends, arguing with her dad, dealing with his own dad. He did all that. Married her. And now she's dead?! And Landon Carter is alone? That's the worst movie I've ever seen."

He had a valid point. It was one of the saddest stories out there. "Ah, fair enough." I said. "But, with great love comes great loss, right?" I walked back over to him and kissed his cheek.

"No way. Not always." He pulled me back onto his lap.

Maybe an hour later, after I'd showered and gotten ready for dinner, again, we left the cottage and walked over to the big house together. With a side dish that we made, together.

"About time you two showed up. While you were in there making out, we all ate." Roy yelled across the backyard. "Who's ready to play some ball?"

"Dude, can it wait?" I said. "It's cold, and we're hungry."

"I bet you are." Port said from his chair on the porch. "Don't worry, I saved you each a plate." I didn't even give him the satisfaction of an answer. I just rolled my eyes as I walked through the door to join the rest of the ladies in the kitchen. I turned around again just in time to see Port hand Hobie a beer. Not a word, but a sign of brotherly love, nonetheless. I leaned against the corner cabinet, out of sight, but directly in ear shot of a conversation that would change my world, or at least remind me of everything I had.

"Do you love her?" Port asked. Blunt as could be.

"It scares the hell out of me, but yes, sir. Yes, I do." Hobie answered. Inside, hiding in the kitchen, my stomach churned with happiness and nerves all at the same time. "And I'm sorry. If that has caused you any trouble here."

"Man, look. You've got a job and a family here for life if you want it, don't ever worry about any trouble. What I'm more interested in is whether you and Ruby have sorted your own mess out yet, because that girl loves you, and I wouldn't be a big brother if I didn't step in to make sure she wasn't going to get her heart broken."

"It's the only thing I'm afraid of, hurting her." I needed him to let go of that. I needed Hobie to trust that we could do this together, and that everything would be okay. I knew it was going to take time, but I really was starting to see it.

"I don't think you have it in you. I don't think you could. Cause it seems to me like you love her too much to ever do something that would break her heart."

My brother knew how to lay it on thick. That's what a big brother is for though, and if there was one thing I could say about Port, it was that he always had my best interest at heart. He could be annoying, he could make a mess out of anything, and you could be sure that he would be embarrassing and mildly inappropriate at the worst of times. But, he had the love of a brother nailed down, and he knew exactly what to do with it.

Hobie didn't really answer him. It seemed like he was thinking, though. But, Port kept on.

"Look. I know you've walked through some tough stuff. To be honest, Ruby hasn't walked through much more than a speed bump. At least not since our aunt passed away. Ruby believes in butterflies and happy endings. She's all peaches and cream and sweet dreams all the time. She doesn't believe in rainy days, or in people letting her down. She's never been hurt so bad that she questioned whether or not the world is good. But you, well it seems to me that the world pretty much showed you it's not much more than shit sometimes. But man, if you'd let her, I think Ruby could show you the other side."

Hobie looked up at Port and almost smiled. "I love her. She's... changed the way I see myself. I want to see the world the way she does."

"Give it time." Port finished his beer. "Good talk, man. And, if you ever need..." I think Port wanted to make sure he didn't cross any lines here. He stopped, and hung his head. "Well, if you ever need a brother, I'm here."

If I'd had any questions left at all about us, Port just took care of it for me. I knew now, without a doubt, that Hobie was a perfect fit. Not just for me, but for my world. My family, the estate, this town. It might have been a bumpy road for him to get here, but if he found the water when he got here, maybe he would finally feel what smooth sailing feels like.

Port stepped into the kitchen, and caught me eavesdropping.

"Did I miss anything?" He asked.

"Pretty much nailed it," I said as I reached up to kiss him on the cheek. "Thank you, Port." He kissed my forehead and took off, yelling at the boys about their video game controllers. Life, and noise, as usual.

I went back out onto the porch, and found Hobie staring out over the marina.

"You take interrogation pretty well." I stepped up beside him, and looked up to find a red eyed man doing his best not to cry. "What is it?" I asked.

"He loves you more than you'll ever know." Hobie said. "Your whole family, this whole place. You guys are like a giant puzzle, that is so intricately designed and cut. And I kind of feel like I'm a piece of that puzzle."

"You are, Hobie. And one day that won't surprise you."

"I know," He laughed. "It feels good."

We didn't leave the property together very often. Someone was always busy working or traveling. Most of the gathering took place right there at home. So it made a double date even more exciting when the boys took Penny and me downtown for a change. We love the island life, but no one complains when you get us somewhere new. We walked in and out of every joint on Front Street, and quickly had entirely too much to eat and were nearing that limit on too much to drink. We were in line for ice cream when it started to rain.

"Why don't we go get the truck and come pick y'all up?" Hobie offered. I leaned up to kiss his cheek.

"You're such a gentleman." Penny shoved Port before offering her two cents. "Isn't he such a gentleman, Port?" She knew how to proverbially kick her husband in the balls. Port was a gentleman, when he wanted to be. But, I think Penny wanted that to be a whole lot more often.

The guys took off toward the docks where we'd left the truck. "It will be at least a half hour before they get back here." I said. "Gives me plenty of time to drink my own milkshake and start on his." I didn't mind the extra time with Penny either. She was my sister in law, and we'd basically been raised like siblings anyway, but Penny was also a really good friend. I never got tired of our time together, and unlike most sisters, she never drove me crazy.

"Seems like things between the two of you are going well." She said, sipping on her milkshake, and nudging her shoulder into mine.

"He's incredible." I answered. "It almost seems too good to be true. Port hires a new guy and he's my perfect match."

"Eh, nothing's perfect." Penny countered.

"Well, no. And I know he isn't, but I think he might just be perfect for me."

"That's what matters." She laughed. "Lord knows your brother isn't perfect, but we have a damn good life together. I wouldn't trade it for the world. For *me*, he is perfect."

"Look at us. All sappy and wife-like."

"I am a wife... so. All's fair." She slurped the ends of her milkshake. "You, on the other hand..." She waved her hand my way, tapping my ring finger.

"Oh stop it. It hasn't been long enough for that."

"I'm just saying. Whenever, wherever. We like him. And we like what he does for you."

"Me too." I was blushing now. We were going to have to change the subject before the boys picked us up. I didn't need to try and explain this conversation to them. I was too busy blushing about my love life, in fact, to notice the headlights that were coming our way. I guess I assumed they would stop. We were in the crosswalk and they had a red light. We had a walking signal. I looked straight at them, and it still didn't occur to me, that they weren't slowing down.

It didn't even hurt at all. Or maybe, they hit us hard enough that I just didn't know how much it hurt.

EIGHTEEN

Hobie

It was all a blur. Having been trained to choose to fight in times like these, I didn't quite understand how to run with flight instead. We went from walking, to the parking garage, to the accident, to the hospital. I had trouble hearing all of it, and for a little while I had trouble remembering it all.

I hadn't really thought about it, not even for a second. When I pulled onto the estate, I'd only left the hospital a few minutes earlier. I must have been driving entirely too fast. Not that I cared. If I'd died right that second, it wouldn't have mattered. To be honest, if I had died right then, it would have been faster than I could have managed to get out of there on my own. It was happening; I was doing exactly what I thought I'd never do again. In fight or flight, I chose flight. I chose weakness.

My heart was beating so hard, and so fast, the entire time I was packing. I could feel my pulse in my fingertips. I could hear it deep in my ears. I'd lost a sense of anything that wasn't in my hands. My clothes as I tossed them into the suitcase. The handle as I slammed the door shut. I didn't take the time to lock anything up. I peeled out of the driveway so fast that I wasn't even sure I had everything. I just left. And it couldn't have been fast enough.

I fell in love. I found a home. I had it all. And then in one night, it all came crashing down exactly the way I was used to. I almost lost her. For a few minutes, I felt it. I felt what it would feel like to lose her. The very thing I was afraid of, the only thing I wanted to avoid, and I'd let it happen. I didn't protect her. Once more, and for the very last time, the person I loved the most had gotten hurt because of me.

I left her. I left her with Penny, in the dark, and the rain. I left them alone. And if I had just stayed, maybe I could have gotten them out of the way. Maybe I could have kept her from getting hit. Hell, she didn't get hit. She got completely run over; rolled and tossed. Ruby, Penny, and a few other people who were crossing the street. That damn truck just knocked them all down, and ran straight over them. By the time we got there, the police were arresting the driver, who was so drunk he didn't even realize he'd caused an accident.

Penny peeled herself up off the street. She was covered in blood, and you couldn't tell where one cut ended and another started. But she stood up and stumbled away.

The only reason Ruby made it into an ambulance is because officers and medics hang around late at night downtown by the most crowded bars, just in case. If she'd had to wait for help, she wouldn't have made it. An officer got to her first and wrapped his hands around her leg where it seemed like most of her blood was coming from. Someone else had taken a shirt and was holding it above her eye. Just as we got close enough to see, they were closing the ambulance doors and rolling away.

"You can follow us to Regional," the medic said as he shut the door.

Port threw me back into the truck and took us straight to the hospital. We'd long lost Ruby's ambulance, but Penny was in the one right in front of us.

I managed to hear a few things as we stood in the waiting room. They were both *stable.* There were broken bones. Scans. Concussions. Trauma. Unimaginable blood loss. We heard someone page a trauma surgeon, and a few nurses yelling about an MRI. I didn't know what any of it meant, and even if I did, I was only hearing bits and pieces. I couldn't put it all together. Looking back, I'm not even sure I was in a clear state of mind. As much as I was trying to slow down and listen, I couldn't keep my mind on any one conversation long enough to understand.

Rhett, Amy, and Eddy came barrelling through the hospital doors and as they all ran to Port, I silently backed out of the room. I walked straight to the truck that we had left by the ambulance doors, got in, and drove away.

Was it shallow of me? Weak? Was I so afraid of what was happening that I couldn't man up and be there for my girl? Yes. Absolutely it was. But it was still the only thing I could do. Running away was the easy way out, and I ran faster than I ever had before.

Highway 17 south. I don't know why, but that's the road I chose. I was just heading for anywhere that this situation didn't exist. Anywhere that I wouldn't have a girlfriend who was dying because I'd walked away.

I hadn't felt this way since the accident when I was deployed. Seeing my unit, dead and injured all around me; that was the last time I remembered feeling so confused. Like I was hearing a million conversations at once, but deaf. I genuinely didn't think I could ever feel like that again. I didn't think I'd survive it. I regretted it immediately, leaving her. But it was the lesser of two wrong choices, and it was the only choice that would give her a fighting chance.

Everyone around me died. I was stupid to think I could live a good life, and it went on for far too long. If she made it, I wouldn't ever risk doing that to her again. I needed to be as far away from her as I could get; far enough that I knew she'd be safe from here on.

The responsibility would always come back to me. If I hadn't said yes to Port and moved to the estate, this wouldn't have happened. If I'd swallowed every last one of those pills and downed the alcohol rather than answer the phone call, no one would have ever gotten hurt because of me again. I was selfish to think I could try to live again.

When I pulled into the city limits of Savannah, my eyes were so swollen from crying that I could hardly see. I was tired, I was confused, and my vision was fading. I stopped at the first hotel I came across, and booked a room. But, by the time I checked in, and tossed my bag on the bed, I decided I needed a drink to settle down. So I drove down the road a bit, and stopped at the first bar I found.

"What brings you to town?" The bartender poured two drinks, just like I asked. Demanded, really. I wasn't exactly polite. He put the two glasses in front of me. Blackberry brandy, on the rocks. Drunk Hobie wouldn't be much different than the Hobie that showed up at this bar. My eyes were already swollen, my mind was already numb, and my social graces were gone. Five hours of wondering what I was thinking, letting anyone get that close to me. What disregard I must have had for her life, knowing that she'd get hurt around me, and then letting it happen.

I didn't look up to him when I answered. "Just driving through." I finished both drinks immediately, and motioned for another round.

"At this rate, you're going to be hanging out here tonight, bud."

"Whatever." I drank the next two. "Bud."

"Look man. You can sleep in your car in the parking lot. Or in the hotel up the street. But if this is what you're doing tonight, then no. You're not driving through. You're staying here."

I threw my keys at him. "Well keep pouring then, *bud*."

He kept pouring, and I kept drinking. Eventually, I flipped my phone over and saw the seventeen missed phone calls from Port, eleven from Penny. One from Rhett. One from Eddy.

Then I made the mistake of opening up the unread text messages, most from Port.

Don't you dare leave her like this.

This is exactly what you swore you wouldn't do. Don't do this to her.

Don't be a coward, Hobie.

This is insane. Hobie. Come back.

Call someone, man. At least let us know you're okay. She is going to wonder where you are. What are we supposed to tell her?

Can you man up and come here, so that you can talk to her yourself?

I don't know what's going through your head, Hobie. Just come back. We're going to fix this. I promise.

And then, just one text from Penny. Graceful, and concerned.

Please, Hobie. Where are you? I'll come for you. Everything will be okay. Come back to us. Please. Come home.

Home. Another reminder that I'd let this all go too far. I shouldn't have let the estate turn into my home. I shouldn't have let the Dixon family, especially Ruby, turn into my family. I shouldn't have let her become mine. I shouldn't have made her think it was safe to love me. I'd let her down in the most unforgivable way.

"Another." I said. Two more glasses appeared in front of me. Water.

"You're done." He said.

"Screw you." I stood up to leave and threw cash on the bar. I could just find another place to drink. I didn't get that far though. I'm not exactly sure that both of my feet made it to the floor before I did. Before my entire body made it to the floor. I remember that part, the falling.

I woke up, immediately wishing I hadn't. Not for guilt, I didn't even remember that much. But for the first few seconds, enough time to blink once or twice, what I was regretting was that I only drank enough to feel like death, and not enough to actually just die.

Maybe a minute later, it occurred to me that I had no idea where I was. Though, the bed was surprisingly comfortable. I was certain that the foul odor was actually me, as drunk as I still felt. The room, through my blurry eyes, was relatively neat and clean.

I sat up, slowly enough but still not sure if my head came with me. After a few deep breaths, I found just enough balance to try to move. I wouldn't have bothered to get up at all if I didn't have to piss so bad. I drug my feet across the wood floors, and to a bedroom door, briefly afraid of what I was going to find on the other side. I hadn't had this much to drink since my brother died. I would have drank myself gone another night, but I ended up at the hospital myself, and, well...

Not that I had any intentions of going back to Ruby. No, I loved her enough that I planned to get as far away as possible. Still, there was a small piece of me that was disgusted with the idea that I might have gone home with some girl last night.

I was oddly pleased to open the bedroom door to a living room, a rather manly living room, and an ogre of a man standing in the kitchen. Tattoos covering almost every inch of his arms and neck, greasy hair tucked under a ball cap. I went home with a dude? Didn't I get a hotel room?

"Sup, bro? Enough room in that cesspool of a stomach for some eggs?" I got nauseous at the thought of food, though, I was also sure that eating was one step to getting myself out of this drunken hell.

I grunted, and sat down on one of the bar stools, letting my face fall into my hands.

"Ah." He answered. "Let's start with toast then. Plain." He put a plate in front of me with two pieces of toast on it. Then he came back with a mug of black coffee, and four tylenol.

"Drink up." He raised his mug at me. "You're good for business, but I'd be willing to bet you wish you hadn't had so much to drink last night."

"Not particularly." I said. "Kind of wish I'd had a few more, actually."

"That bad, huh?"

"No disrespect, uh..." I didn't know his name.

"Austin." He reached out to shake my hand. It took every fibre of my being to do so. "Most people call me Auss."

"Bartender?" I asked.

"Bar owner, actually. But yes, a bartender too, at least a few nights a week."

"Hobie." I said. "Sorry. If I... well. Sorry."

"No problem, Hobie. Roommate just got married and moved out. So, you got lucky really. Figured I wasn't about to let you drive off anywhere. But you took care of that one for me when you passed out on the floor. Toph over there—" He pointed over toward the couch, where another tattooed arm lifted up and waved. "reminded me that we had the spare room. Said you looked like a reasonable dude having an unreasonable day. So. Here you are."

"Well. That makes more sense." I wasn't sure what I had thought happened, but drunkenly going home with two large and burly tattooed men wasn't exactly on my list of possibilities.

"So. I'm Auss. That's Toph. You're Hobie. Now that we're all on the same page, why'd you come here trying to drink yourself through the pearly gates last night?"

"Wouldn't have been the pearly gates, more like wrought iron on fire. Someone got hurt because of me, and that can't happen anymore. So, I took off. Figure I need to get far away from her, and go somewhere I can find enough to drink, or some place to live. Alone." I swallowed the tylenol and sipped a bit more of the coffee. I had to buck up some bravery to try the toast.

Auss looked up as Toph got up from the couch, and walked over to the bar stool next to me. After a few seconds of looking at eachother like they had a hidden agenda, I started to get concerned again. Not that I thought a couple murdering brutes would have offered me coffee and breakfast.

Whatever they were mind reading to each other, Toph finally spoke up.

"Your tattoo, on your neck. What's that?"

I reached up to touch my neck, needing to think for a second about which tattoo he was referring to. Ah, it was the anchor. A plain black anchor, with *semper fidelis* inside.

"Marine Corps. Been a few years." I muttered.

"That's what I thought. Hence, the relatively comfortable place to sleep. You're welcome by the way."

"Thank you." I looked back over to Toph. "Why do you ask?"

Toph lifted his tee shirt sleeve to reveal a tattoo on his shoulder. Among other things, I was able to see the trident, and the year 2006. "SEALS. Not that we usually go around shouting that from the rooftops, but, we saw your drunk ass and figured maybe we'd cut you some slack."

Auss put up three plates at the bar top and then grabbed a fork and dug in. I was still trying to convince my stomach that breakfast was an option. "Well then. Now that we know we were right in our assumptions. You can crash here if you need. So long as whatever you're running away from isn't going to get us into any legal trouble or anything. I'll do anything but harbor a fugitive. But seriously, there's an empty spare room if you need it. And we happen to need a little bit of help downstairs in the bar. So. You need it, it's yours. Say the word."

Did I really get drunk with a couple strangers and end up with a new place to live and a new job? What is this life I was stumbling through? I'd spent a lot of time thinking I'd have died by now, wishing for it, really. Instead, I keep managing to hurt everyone, and skate out into a new opportunity. What the hell was wrong with me?

"Ok. Well. I guess I could do that. I have no idea what I'm doing now."

"Well, feel free to keep on... running. Or whatever it is you're doing." Toph said with a mouthful.

"Just getting away from a mess I caused. I can hang out for a few weeks." I finished off the piece of toast and went for a bite of eggs, but laid the fork back down.

"You smell like ass. Maybe try eating again after a shower or something." Auss pointed to the bathroom.

"Thanks."

NINETEEN

Ruby

"Hey, girl."

Port's voice always created a safe place for me, and I'd recognize it anywhere. Even here, among all the other noises that were so loud and so muffled at the same time. My eyes hurt. Everything hurt. The pressure in my head was too much when I first tried to look for him. I reached up to my face, but I felt his hand squeeze mine and bring it back down to the bed.

"They said everything might be blurry for a while, until the swelling goes down. But I'm right here. Right next to you."

I tried to grab onto his hand again, but it hurt.

"Where is he?" I begged at a whisper.

"Ruby. Let's just worry about you, okay?"

"Pen?" I croaked.

"She's okay." I felt him readjust his grip on my hand. "Mom and dad took her back to the house a few hours ago. Bumps and bruises, mostly. I told them I'd wait here with you."

"Where's Hobie?" I asked again.

"I don't know, Ruby. I'm sorry. He's okay. He was here, but he, I think he took off. He won't answer my calls."

"Not his fault." It hurt to speak, but I had to figure out a way to tell him. He had to know. "Tell him." I tried to sit up, and realized I couldn't.

"Ruby, I know it's not his fault." He wasn't just agreeing with me. I knew in his tone that he believed it too. We both knew it wasn't Hobie's fault, and I think we both knew that's how he would see it anyway.

"Tell him." I managed to get a little louder. Something started beeping, an alarm maybe. Port stood from his chair and sat on the edge of the bed next to me.

"Okay, Ruby. You have to calm down." He helped me to settle back down onto the bed and pulled a blanket up over my shoulders. "Just rest. Okay? I'll tell him. It's not his fault. I'll tell him."

I think I fell asleep after that. Or maybe I passed out. I don't really know.

A few days went by in the hospital, and I'd graduated to eating a little bit at a time, and moving from the bed to the chair and back a few times a day. Somehow, I'd gotten run over by a truck, and managed to only have one broken leg. Everything else was just impact wounds; one major set of stitches above my eye, a few just behind my ear, and apparently quite a bit more in the cast on my leg. The rest was just swelling. I could handle that. I would heal. Would he?

A week later, I was being pestered by physical therapists three times a day to walk the hallway. It drove me nuts, but apparently that was the ticket home. After a week's worth of those three-a-days, I was discharged. The walking, and I think quite a bit of begging on my own behalf, and probably the pestering from my brother. It all worked together, I felt relief for the first time, taking in the view as Port pulled into the driveway on the estate. I'd never been so glad to be home.

Port and my dad had set up the downstairs master suite for me to stay in at the big house. It was closer to them than my own cottage, and it didn't have any stairs for me to deal with while I recovered.

I got out of the truck in the driveway and turned to look toward the gardens to the cafe and my house on Cottage Row.

"Ruby, come on." Port said.

"I'm just looking." I said. "I can stay there, you know. I could manage."

"I think you should stay out of there for a while."

"Because Hobie left me here?" I said. He hung his head; and he knew I was right. "Fair enough." He was only trying to protect me.

I wiped a few tears from my cheek. It wasn't worth trying to hide them. It did sting a little, emotionally and physically, wiping them from my bruised face.

This would all be fine for a few days, but they were going to have to back off a little. I really just wanted to be alone.

Dad stayed just long enough to fix me a plate for lunch, and Port got me settled onto the couch with the remote controls, and a month's worth of snacks and drinks.

"I'll be back in a few hours. You're due for pain pills at two." Port said, standing at the front door. "Can I bring you anything?"

"No, thank you." I wasn't feeling too chatty. As glad as I was to be out of that hospital, I can't say that I was glad to be here, now that I knew for sure that home was without Hobie. Port had already told me he was gone, but part of me hoped that we would get home and he would be there. A misunderstanding maybe, just a quick break. Of course, we came home and he was really gone.

How could he do that? How could he leave me? Surely he knew that this wasn't his fault.

But how could he leave?

TWENTY

Hobie

I'd been helping the guys out in the bar for a few weeks. The job paid with a place to stay, food to eat, and no commitments. Free time was spent either alone, or with the guys. They left me well enough alone though, so I didn't mind it. Sure, they were basically strangers, but we'd gotten along well. I think that was a guy thing, the ability to just get along and do the work that needed to be done. The rest was a Marine thing; a team's a team no matter what, no matter how well you do or do not know each other.

I was missing the work on the estate, and missing her. The bar was busy enough at night time that the hours went by pretty fast, but during the day I found myself wishing I was working the stables. I was wondering what I could be getting done at the marina, and how the day was going on the Erv. I wanted to drop by the cafe. I wanted to kiss her. I missed my girl.

I knew it before, but being away like this was a clear reminder. As much as I swore I wouldn't allow myself to feel like I belonged, as much as I hated to realize it, I'd come to feel completely at home on the estate. Now that I was gone, I felt like I was in the wrong place, like I had somewhere to go back to. But I knew that I had to leave. The only way to help Ruby get better, and keep her safe from now on, was to be as far away from her as possible. It didn't feel right, and it certainly wasn't easy. Missing her hurt more than anything, but I couldn't figure out a better solution. I truly didn't believe that there was one.

Don't get me wrong. It didn't take leaving to see what I had there. I knew all along that I had it good, that I had more than I deserved. It didn't take leaving to see that. It just took leaving to feel it; and it wasn't a feeling I'd be able to hold for long. Admittedly, I wasn't the strongest guy when it came to my emotions. Loneliness, no matter how much of it I caused myself, was a lot. The depth of having a lot of love to give, but no one to give it to—and then having people to love, but being afraid to try—it was a lot to think through. As much as I wanted to put the hurt away, that was hard too. You'd think I'd have been the master of loneliness at this point, but that's something that never really got easier.

For some salt in the wound, Christmas came at warp speed. The hours went by at a painfully slow pace, but somehow six weeks went by. For a little while in the early morning of Christmas Eve, I got caught up in the idea of going back to the estate. I couldn't imagine spending Christmas here, away from

Ruby; away from the family. But as painful as it was, I couldn't do it. I tried to put my things in my bag. I thought about gassing up the truck and heading north to Wrightsville. What caught me was thinking about what I'd say to her when I got there. I wondered if she'd even be willing to talk to me. I knew I had hurt her. I couldn't blame her if she didn't want to see me ever again. Let alone the damage I'd caused with Port and my job, or lack thereof.

Christmas at the bar was an easy day. I slept in until lunch, and ate a peanut butter sandwich. I even had some chocolate milk, just to keep things festive. Then I opened up the bar. Auss and Toph had gone home for the day, so it was just me and the alcohol. It didn't seem like too much of a responsibility, bartending on Christmas. Who would want to spend Christmas day in a bar?

Turns out, there are quite a few lonely people in Savannah. Within five minutes after unlocking the doors, the bar top was full of people, all who had arrived alone, and within the hour they were all socializing and having a great time together. It was interesting really, the way a whole bunch of lonely people showed up and spent a holiday together. None of them seemed lonely anymore. It had me wondering if this wouldn't be such an awful way to spend my life afterall. I could handle being alone most of the time, and if it ever got to be too quiet, I could find myself in a place like this enjoying some time with strangers until I was ready to be alone again.

Time with strangers here and there I could handle. That seemed safe. Staying somewhere long term, letting people in, letting myself feel like I had a family, that was out of the question. But I could tend to a bar, be a listening ear for the traveling soldier or the visitor here and then who needed to talk through their own life. At the end of the night, they'd be on their way, and I'd be nothing more than someone they babbled their story to for a few hours. No love. No connection. No desperate attempts at a relationship.

Actually, that was the beginning of a turning point. It occurred to me that, for the most part, if someone came here to the bar alone to get through their loneliness, somehow they left like the problem had been solved. They would come and sit, shoot the bull with whoever was behind the bar, work through whatever was going on in their head, and then get back to it.

Part of me wondered if the week or so after slicing my hand open with a glass may have served a similar purpose. Something went wrong, and I had something to work through. For the first time in years, I had people who were ready to work through it with me. I had someone on the other side of the bar, listening, and helping me to sort through next steps. Instead of finishing a conversation, and going home to try again, I ran out on the tab. I left the family, the girl, who cared enough to help, and ran out on the tab.

She came for me. She came to the house, and begged me to let her in. Port took me to the hospital, and begged me to let them in. In a way, I did. I went back to the estate, and got back to work. I opened up with Ruby, and stuck around long enough to get past it. I was faced with fight or flight, and I chose to fight. I had grown, and took it for granted. Things got hard again, and rather than fight through it like I was capable of, I ran.

Things slowed down, and a few hours went by with no new visitors. Everyone had mostly taken off, and I was just sitting around, listening to music and cleaning up. The bells chimed at the door, and I looked up to find an old familiar soul standing there in the doorway, roughing up his boots on the mat before walking across the bar toward me.

"Merry Christmas, boy." Eddy walked in and Rhett followed right behind him. I guess I'd paused in shock, because suddenly Eddy was reaching across the bar to shake my hand as he sat down. Rhett next, shook my hand and sat down, acting as if no time had passed at all.

"Didn't think we'd see any neon lights on today." Rhett chuckled. "Can't complain about a good beer on Christmas day, though."

"How'd y'all know I was here?" I asked.

"Well, Ruby started mumbling about some weekend the two of you spent down here. She hasn't been eating so well. I asked her what might get her to eat lunch with me, and she said I'd have to come all the way down here to get some kind of fancy burger." Eddy laughed.

"You came here for a burger?" I asked, opening a bottle.

"No, dumbass." Rhett said. "The burger in Savannah was a clue. Didn't take us too long to wonder if you might have been thinking about her too, hiding down here at your romantic weekend getaway."

It made sense, though I hadn't really considered that she may have been why I ran here in the first place. I could feel her here. If I closed my eyes I could see her, safe, and loving me.

"Leave it to me, to find you here in the first bar I chose. Gotta say though, I'm a little shocked to find you on the pouring side. What are you doing?" Eddy cut right to it.

I grabbed a glass and poured him a whiskey over two ice cubes. "Just the way I like it." He raised his glass to me. "Thank you."

"How are you guys doing?" I popped the top off a Sam Adams Boston Lager for Rhett, grabbed a stool and sat down across from them.

"Well, we're fine, son. But we didn't come here to talk about us." Eddy took a sip and swirled his glass.

"You don't have to worry about me. I'm alright."

"You are not." Rhett said. "Don't you lie to me. And no one said we were here for you anyhow, but while we're on the subject, let's go ahead and address it. Why'd you take off like that?"

"Rhett..." I sighed. "I'm sorry. Really. You don't—" He raised his finger at me.

"No. You don't get to weasel out of this one. It's time for us to talk about this, man to man." In all fairness, Rhett had every right in the world to take me on. And I deserved it. "Now, I know it took you some time to warm up, and jump in back home. I know you had your hesitations about everyone. But I also know that you love Ruby more than any of us realized. And she went and fell in love with you a bit more than she knew was possible."

Eddy set his glass down and cut in. "What I can't figure out, is why you're willing to let all of that go, because of something crazy that wasn't even your fault."

"I wasn't driving, Eddy, but believe me, I'm the reason that happened. Everyone around me gets hurt. It's how it's always been. I left her and Penny, and they got hurt. I didn't need a reminder that people aren't safe around me, but that was a clear one."

Someone else came into the bar, and I got up to get them a drink. When I came back, it looked like Eddy had been thinking.

"What is it, man. You look stumped." I said, sitting back down.

"I'm not going to fight with you about who's at fault for a stupid accident. You're wrong, I'm right, and you'll figure that out eventually. I'm also older and wiser, and I've got something to say to you, so listen here." He finished off his drink, and I stood up to pour him another.

Rhett stopped me. "No, we don't need another. We're going to get some food and then go home to our family, because it's Christmas."

"Fair enough." I filled two glasses with water.

"I found her, when I was young, even younger than you. Our life was too easy, too perfect." Eddy started.

"Nori." I said.

"Nori." He went on. "Now, I know you know a bit about her. Ruby, she's got a lot of Nori in her." He looked to Rhett and laughed. "Funny, they don't share an ounce of blood, and they didn't even have much time together. But somehow, Ruby has every good quality Nori had."

"Nori must have been incredible. Ruby... she's perfect." I said.

"You're damn right she is." Rhett said. "And she knew it, too. Until you walked out on her."

I sat and listened, guilty. Eddy waved to settle him down.

"Let me tell you something about perfect, son. It doesn't come around every day. Not everyone gets perfect. Lord knows you didn't, not at first. Not the second or third time around either, from what I gather. But I wonder, if maybe something perfect found its way to you, because you already went through hell and back. Maybe you deserve perfect, because you've done your time."

"I can't risk that. Eddy. She is perfect, and she's perfect for me. But I can't risk hurting her."

"What do you think she's feeling right now then, with you here?" Rhett said. "You think she feels good about this? You think she isn't hurting? Look at you. It's obviously hurting you, too."

"Guys. I—"

"I'm not done." Eddy raised a finger to me again, obviously well rehearsed in the art of giving a fatherly lecture. "I had perfect, and it got ripped away from me. I married her. I had a family with her, and I lost her, and it was painful—but Hobie..." I saw his eyes well up with tears. I could feel the pain radiating from deep within his bones. He swallowed the lump in his throat. "Hobie. I wouldn't trade a single second of the time we did have together, to avoid the pain of losing her. It was worth it. Having her, having a love like that, it was worth the pain I feel now, having lost her. You can't run away from a good thing because you're afraid you might lose it. The only good thing I have left... is everything she gave me. This family. This life. It's all because I *did* have her."

I wiped the back of my hand across my eyes, before I tried to answer. I knew he was right, I just didn't know if I had it in me to trust that and run with it. I felt like a sorry excuse of a man, and she deserved better than that.

"I've lost so much already. I can't lose her, too." Here I was, a grown man, sobbing to two old men in a bar.

"Well by running away, by hiding here, you're making damn sure that you do lose her. Why not come home and just enjoy the fact that you *have* her. Whatever might come of it."

"She won't want me. Why would she want me after I did this to her? I left her."

"Boy, that girl is miserable. All she's ever believed in was love like I had. I honestly didn't think she'd ever let herself love like she loves you; I kind of thought she was going to hold the world to such high standards that she'd pass on the good stuff. But damn if you didn't show up and meet those standards. She had it, and she lost you, and she's miserable. I know exactly what that feels like. The difference is that you can fix it for her. You can come back. So come home. Come back to her."

"I'm sorry," I stuttered. "I hurt your family."

"Hobie." Rhett lifted a hand to my shoulder. "We love you. We all do. And it does hurt, you being gone. Because there's... well there's a hole in our family where you should be. You may not have grown up with us, but Hobie, there was clearly always a spot in our home for you. We were just waiting for you to come along. And now, son, if you just come back, I think maybe we can get through all this together. You might just learn that Ruby, and your home, it's been waiting for you all this time. You make it all complete. You make *her* complete."

Not that any of this was the typical way a family worked, but the way Rhett and Eddy treated me, from day one, was not what I ever expected from the family of the girl I loved. They treated me like their own son from the very beginning. I wanted to be that kind of friend, and that kind of dad one day.

They stood up and tossed cash on the bar, which I slid right back to them.

"Merry Christmas, son." Rhett said. They walked to the door and stopped as Eddy turned back to me.

"Oh, and one other thing. The world is what's broken, son—not you. We'll see you when you get home."

And with a nod and a wave, they left. They didn't give me a chance to respond, they just walked out the door like fairy godfathers at midnight. The bells chimed as the door closed, and I sulked back down onto the bar stool. The song that came over the speakers just then was almost like a final smack across the face that they were right. I needed to go home.

I completely lost myself, crying at that bar, as I listened to the words.

When you get home, she'll start to cry. When she says I'm sorry, say so am I. And look into those eyes so deep in love, and drink it up. Because that's the good stuff.

Kenny Chesney sure knew how to kick a guy right in the heart. Maybe he was right. Maybe the good stuff was worth losing it in the end. Maybe having it at all was worth the fear of losing her. Whether I went home or not, I knew now that Ruby would be the only good stuff I'd have for the rest of my life. I wouldn't have anything if I didn't have her.

Okay, I had to go home.

I spent another half hour or so cleaning up the bar, getting ready for Auss and Toph to get back. They'd spent most of the day with their families, but were coming back tonight to close down the bar. I'd been here a while now, and the shift switching had gotten pretty smooth. Between the three of us, the place was almost always covered. I guess they really did need the help, and I seemed to fit in pretty easily.

I looked up as I heard the bells chime again, and the guys poured into the place loud as can be; all holly and jolly and festive. "Hobie! Man! Merry Christmas! How are things here at the north pole?"

"Merry Christmas, guys. It's been a good day. Got a little loud around lunch time, but it's been quiet ever since." I tossed the keys to Auss. "Look, uh." That's as far as I got.

"Ahhhhh." He said, sitting down at the bar while Toph came around and poured a few drinks. "Let me guess. You finally got your head out of your ass, and decided you are ready to go get your girl."

"Well you could have been a bit nicer about that, Auss." Toph spoke up, before looking back to me. "Okay, but really man. Are you done hiding here? She probably misses you." He mocked me with his hand to his heart and batting his eyes at me.

"Are you two ganging up on me?" I laughed.

"Yes." They answered.

"Hey, it's a real Christmas miracle!" Auss added.

"I think it's time for me to take off," I admitted.

"Well, thanks for your help around here man. Guess we'll have to get back to looking for a new hire." He rolled his eyes.

The bells chimed again and I looked across the bar to see another familiar face, roughing his boots on the mat and walking over to the bar.

"Hobie. Gentleman." Port nodded to the guys.

"Port? Merry Christmas." He stepped up and gave me a hug.

"Merry Christmas. Look I'm going to cut straight to it." I put my hands up between us to stop him.

"Don't." I said. "I know."

"You do?" He asked.

"Yes. Rhett and Eddy already gave me a full talking-to."

"Here?" He looked surprised.

"All the elves know how to find the north pole." Auss laughed. I found myself debating if he was sober enough to run the bar the rest of the day. What kind of drinks were served at their Christmas dinners, anyway?

"Yes. They just left, maybe an hour ago. But listen. I wanted to ask you, if maybe my job on the estate would still be available. Unless of course, you've already filled the position."

Port rolled his eyes and shrugged his shoulders. "Oh thank God." he said. "I thought I was going to have to come here and convince you. Or beg or something."

"No begging necessary. Can I come back, man? Can I come home?"

"Please, dude. She's miserable. And I have no intentions of handling that property by myself. I need you to come back. Also... I miss my friend." He stood up. "Does this mean we can get in the car and go? I really don't want to miss dessert. If we don't go soon, the cinnamon rolls are going to be gone by the time we get back."

"Tell you what." I said, looking to Auss and Toph who were both just sitting there like they were watching a movie. "Hit the road, enjoy your night. Just give me some time. I'll see you there."

"Deal." He shook hands with the guys. "Nice to meet y'all. Thanks for keeping our guy here occupied while he did all this thinking." He waved his hands like my thinking was some kind of hocus-pocus.

"No problem." Toph answered. "We needed the help. If y'all are ever in town for a visit, stop by. We need to meet this girl that has Hobie here all twisted around."

"Yeah! She got any sisters?" Auss asked, even merrier than before.

"Just me, big man. Sorry." Port answered, heading back out the door. I guess technically, Penny's sister, Jana, was still up for grabs, but I hadn't even met her, so I kept my mouth shut.

"Bummer." Auss collapsed back onto the bar stool.

"Thanks, man." I shook Auss's hand. "I'll come back and visit sometime soon. I'll bring Ruby. That is, if she's willing to take me back after this."

Auss laughed and kicked me out. I ran back upstairs to the spare room and tossed my things in the bag. The few things I did bring, mostly clothes, packed up easily and before I knew it, I was in the car and on the road; the road home, back to my girl. There was one stop I had to make first, and it was a little out of the way. I sent Port a text message, letting him know I'd be home in a day or two.

I pulled into Toddy Stables, just outside of Louisville, Kentucky. I'd inquired about the horses a while back when Ruby had mentioned adding a few to the stables, and it turned out that a Christmas week fundraiser for the local elementary school was the last day the horses were scheduled for any events. They were going to be advertised for adoption after the first of the year.

When I pulled onto the property, I backed the trailer I'd rented against the stable gates. An older gentleman came out of the barn, removing his hat and shaking my hand.

"Mr. Logan?" He asked.

"Yes, sir. Nice to meet you. Please, call me Hobie."

"Thanks for coming here so soon. We're glad to see these two go to such a good home. We've heard good things about the Ervin property."

"Yes sir. I'm excited to get them home. I think they'll love it there. Plenty of room to run, a couple old guys to live with, and a really pretty girl who's been excited to meet them." Just the thought brought a smile to my face.

We walked into the barn and he took me straight to their gate. They looked incredible. I was excited to bring them back to the estate, though I was a bit worried that Port was going to kick my ass when he realized what I'd done. But, Ruby was on the lookout for these two, and I wanted to bring them home.

"We sure are going to miss them. My wife and I are getting up there. It's getting harder every season to take care of everything and everyone around here. As much as we hate to say goodbye, I think it's best for them if we send them somewhere they can have a lot more attention. These guys might outlive us, I figure." He did look a little down about saying goodbye.

"Well, if there's one thing I can assure you, it's that there's no shortage of attention back home. When you're there, you're family. Whether you like it or not." I laughed, and that seemed to take a bit of the pressure off. "I hope you'll come visit if you ever find yourself heading our way. You're always welcome." That was enough to make the old man smile.

It took about two hours, but we got the horses loaded up into the trailer, and got everything ready for the drive. I wrote the man a check, and got back into my truck. With any luck, by dinnertime, Stout and Morrison here would be pulling up to their new home. And with a bit more luck, Ruby would be excited to see them, *and me*, when we got there.

With a quick wave to the Toddy Stables staff, I pulled out of the driveway and headed home.

TWENTY-ONE

Ruby

Tigua and Sampson had been pretty patient with me. I'd spent each morning with them since I got the cast off my leg and traded it in for a walking boot, but I still wasn't doing as much as I used to. I certainly wasn't ready to ride like I used to. Thankfully, Sam and Roy were managing to get enough done that the stables were in relatively good shape. Port helped with the heavy lifting, and Penny would take them out for a ride most days.

For the first week or so home from the accident, no one really talked about it. I knew I wasn't myself, and I knew it was affecting my family. But I didn't know what to do about it. Even if I did, I didn't care enough to try.

Eventually, the whole herd trying to take care of me at the same time got overwhelming enough that I snapped. Thankfully, that happened while the boys were in school.

Looking back, I know that the adults in my family could forgive me for the things I said. But I'd never forgive myself if I'd said or done anything that was too much for Sam and Roy to understand. This whole thing was too much for them to understand, and I think they were doing better with it all than anyone expected.

Penny laid low with me at first, but she's a mom and—no surprise to anyone—was back up and running well before she was supposed to. Port, Dad, and Uncle Eddy had taken over the kids, the house, and the rest of the property, and everyone else in town stepped up to help out a bit. But at the end of the day everything was all wrong. The balance was off and although Hobie being gone was really just like old times, there was nothing about it that was familiar, or welcome, at all.

When Penny jumped back into the routine, the boys settled down and the ebb and flow of the place fell back into it's normal pace. That was good for everyone, and had it's added benefits for me because it forced everyone to get back to life and stop bugging me.

Every few days, Uncle Eddy took me back over to the house to see what he was working on. Little things here and there were coming together but I hadn't told him much about what I wanted to do with the place since the accident, so mostly he was just keeping it all together until I was ready. I knew I'd get back to it eventually, but for the time being I was doing just fine in the downstairs suite in the big house.

Port took me out on the boat now and then, claiming he needed a hand out on the Erv. But I knew it was just an excuse to get me out of the house, and it worked. Slowly, our short walks from the big house to the docks turned into longer walks to the cafe. And one morning, just before Christmas, Port took me to the beach with our surfboards. He sat with me in the sand and didn't say too much, but he didn't need to. My brother had been with me every step of this wretched journey, and this was just... the next step.

The waves were flat that morning, which was probably for the best since I hadn't been on my board in months, and didn't exactly have the strength to hold my own. I followed him out and turned around, sitting to face the place I called home. It didn't feel like home these days, and I wasn't sure it ever would again.

"One good ride, Ruby. That's all you need. It will help, you'll see."

I nodded, knowing he was right. But part of me still felt like it wasn't worth it. Surfing wasn't going to fix my problems. Some quality time with my brother wasn't going to make the darkness disappear. But eventually I realized we were already out here. Whether I got in by swimming or surfing, I'd have to get back in somehow. Might as well ride.

I remember the wave; I can still see it. The water was almost completely flat the whole time we were out there. But, I could see it coming off in the distance. Just enough of a wave that

I thought the ocean might just be listening after all. And Port was right, it was all I needed.

I turned, paddled into it, and rode right into everything I was craving deep in my bones. I could feel again.

Port rode in right behind me. I stepped off my board and began to cry as I realized the same thing I'd explained to Hobie was coming back full circle for me. I didn't want to drown in this anymore. I didn't want the weight of the world to wash me away. I wanted to float. I wanted to ride on top of it all, and challenge gravity every time it tried to knock me off. I inhaled, immediately overcome with emotion that I could breathe again.

I took a few steps up from the water onto the sand and collapsed to my knees, sobbing. Port sat next to me and pulled me in. No matter what happened next, I knew that I was safe here in my brother's arms. And then I remembered the words Hobie used to explain what it felt like when the tide that drowned him for so long suddenly felt like grace.

It's like no matter what you're carrying, no matter how heavy you feel, it's like you can come back here and let it go.

It was in that exact moment that I understood. The tide would come and go, but the same tide that swept me out to sea would always bring me home. I knew then that I would be okay, and Hobie would, too. He would remember the grace that he'd already found. He just needed to come back here to see it. He just needed to come home.

That was the day that I first tried to get back into my routine. I went back to the cafe to get my hands reacquainted with the chaos. It was the first bit of quality time I'd spent with my mom, and she didn't say a word. She didn't need to. She kissed my head like she always did, and poured me a cup.

I started to talk with Uncle Eddy again about the house. It was time for me to get out of Port's place and back into my own. I was ready for some privacy and some quiet time again. I was surprised when he took me back over there to see that he'd had it move-in ready for quite some time.

"You can always come home, sweetheart. A good home is always ready to welcome you back. It's been here all along."

One by one, I checked things off the list of routines and habits I'd let go of. I wasn't quite as caught up as I needed to be, but I was even starting to think ahead for the stables again. Working out in the barn by myself had given me plenty of time to think, and one thing I was sure of now, was that it was time to bring home some new horses.

I knew that somewhere out there was a horse that didn't just need a home, but needed *this one*. There was a horse that needed *me*. I decided that it was time to talk to Port about it, but someone beat me to it.

I was closing up the doors to the barn that afternoon when I heard the rumble on the gravel road behind me. It was the week after Christmas, and we weren't expecting anyone. Plus, everyone was already home.

The mixture of emotions that flooded me when I saw his truck was almost too much. My face went numb, my fingers shook, and my eyes were already watering at just the sight of Hobie coming down the driveway. I knew that was his truck, but I was surprised to see the trailer.

I stood in place at the barn doors, leaning against the porch post as he pulled up. He circled around so that the trailer was right in front of me at the door. I wiped my eyes when he opened the door. He stood there, hesitant, and looked at me like he didn't know what to do or say. In all fairness, neither did I. So I started by avoiding it altogether.

"What do you have here?" I asked, looking up to the trailer.

"Well. Stout and Morrison. They were on that farm in Kentucky, and I figured since I was coming home, I'd give them a ride." He took a few steps my way.

"You what?" I walked up to the trailer, shocked, and reached for the handle. He stood nearby as I opened the trailer, and stepped up inside. They were beautiful. They had obviously been very well taken care of. To the best of my knowledge, these were two horses that had spent most of their time on the racetrack, but were now retired and ready to spend the rest of their lives on a cushy estate with plenty to eat and room to roam until they were old and cranky.

"Hobie, they're beautiful." I stepped up to pet one of them. "Which one's which?"

"This one is Stout." He pet Stout on the nose and then stepped over to me, standing right behind me and reaching up to grab the ropes on the other horse. "This is Morrison. He's a loud one." He laughed, reaching up to adjust the ropes again. "Threw quite the temper tantrum when I was trying to get him into the trailer. He stomped his feet and yelled at me the whole way home, too. Mr. Toddy said that was pretty standard for him."

"I think we could use a little spunk around here." I said.

Each of us took a set of reins, and led the boys out of the trailer and over toward the barn. We tied their ropes to the fence and let them stretch out a bit. I climbed up onto the top of the fence, and looked at Hobie. He came closer slowly, almost as if he didn't know if he could, like he needed permission.

"Are you here to bring the horses, or are you here to come home?" I asked. As much as I wanted to wrap myself in him and never let go, I was hesitant. It hurt me that he had left. I didn't want to get ahead of myself, if he wasn't going to stay. I held the lump in my throat, praying that the answer he gave me would be the right one.

"I wanted to bring the horses... home to you. I wanted to tell you that I'm sorry." He stepped up next to me, leaning against the fence. "I'm so sorry. I shouldn't have left, and I know that. I just didn't know what to do." He scrunched his face quickly, looking at his feet, like he was trying to keep himself from crying.

"Why did you go?" I asked. "You have to know that it wasn't your fault." I reached for his chin, making him look back up to me.

"It felt like it, though. It still does. I left you. I left you and Penny on your own, and I wasn't there to protect you." I turned a bit toward him, and pulled him closer so that he was standing between my knees, up against the fence.

"Hobie. I know you were scared, but we could have gotten through it together."

"I know... and I'm sorry. I'm so sorry that I hurt you." He brought his hands up to my waist, and dropped his head down. He looked so guilty, so hurt.

"Look at me." I begged him, lifting his face again. "Hobie, look at me." I could tell it took everything he had to bring his eyes to mine, like he was preparing for the worst. "The only thing that I can't handle, is losing you. So whatever it is that we have to deal with, as long as you're willing to stick around, and do it *with me*, Hobie we can get through it. We can handle anything—but you have to stay." He reached up to wipe tears from my cheek. "You have to stay with me. Nothing makes sense without you here, and leaving will never fix anything."

"I love you, Ruby."

"I love you, too." He wrapped his arms around my waist and kissed me as I sat on the fence. I'd forgotten how perfectly we fit together, but I'd never forget the feeling again. The man I loved was right here on the estate, back where he belonged, with me, with our two new horses.

"I messed up," he said. "And I probably will mess up again, more times than you'd probably wish for."

"That's the grace, Hobie. You found the grace. The same tide that drowned you all that time is the one that brought you home."

He smiled and kissed me again, before reaching back up to pet Stout and Morrison.

"Port didn't really want more horses. He's going to kill you." I laughed.

"Eh. You and me and these two. The four of us will be good for this place. He'll see. Besides, it was time for me to pay it forward. You rescued me, brought me home here. I figured it wouldn't be a bad idea if we brought them home here too. Everyone should know what this place is like."

"I could not agree with you more." I said, kissing him again. He lifted me off the fence, and I wrapped my legs around his waist, and my arms around his neck. If there was a way to get close to him, I found it, and I never wanted to let go. "Please tell me you're home for good."

"Home for good." He said. "Actually, I had another idea about that too." He nodded over toward Cottage Row. "I want to help you with the house. I want you to live with me in the guest house while we renovate your place. And then I want you and me to live there together, like a family."

"You want to be my family?" I smiled.

"Ruby, I want to be your whole world. I want to be your husband, your ranch hand, your baby daddy."

"Babies, huh?" I laughed.

"One day. We'll be here with a big family of our own. We'll have it all."

"You want to be my husband?" My stomach flipped with butterflies.

"I do, but we've got things to do first. I'm going to marry you Ruby Dixon. Someday soon. I'm already planning on it, and I'm already planning on you saying yes. So I think maybe we should get to work on that house, and when you're ready, when we're ready, we can get married and move in there together and have babies and—"

I shut him up by kissing him so fast I couldn't even take a breath between his rambling and his lips. Everything was right again. I felt joy. I felt peace. I saw him smile, and I knew that he was home, here on the estate, home with me.

We put the horses into the field and closed the gate behind them. We spent a few hours getting their stables all set up, and then we packed up, getting ready to head back to the house.

"What do you say to a hot shower, a big dinner, and then movie night. Just you and me." he asked.

"Can I pick the movie?"

"Only if you pick *A Walk To Remember*." He winked.

"Obviously." I kissed his cheek and pulled him along, heading back to the house—our house—heading home.

EPILOGUE
Ruby

"Royal and Sampson Dixon!" Penny's voice traveled easily across the property, gracing our ears on the front porch of the guest house. They looked at each other and nodded; silently teaming up for whatever whooping they were about to receive.

"What did y'all do?" I asked. My sister-in-law didn't yell much, but when she did, with their full names, I knew it was serious. Last time, they'd left the gates open, and someone found Tigua down by the ferry dock, kicking one of the cars in the parking lot. The time before that, Roy lit a trash can on fire at the beach, which lit the dune on fire, which traveled the whole way up Frank's pier before the fire department got there to put it out.

"Who knows." Sam grumbled as he stood up and made his way off the porch. I watched as they took their time walking back over to the main house to find their fate.

Hobie and I had talked about having kids recently, but watching Sam and Roy always served as a reminder of what we'd be in for. Just last month Hobie and I decided we weren't talking about kids again until we were at least engaged, preferably married for a year or two—but, what's that saying? If you want to hear God laugh, tell him your plans. Hobie stepped out the front door, set a fresh cup of coffee on the table beside me, and kissed me on the cheek.

"Morning, gorgeous." He said, joining me.

"Sam and Roy are on their way for a reckoning." I laughed, taking a sip.

"Ohhhh, I'd bet she found out about the buoy." He gritted his teeth.

"I'm afraid to ask."

"Yeah, you should be. Let's just hope we have girls. Sweet, kind, peaceful, perfect little girls." He looked at me and we laughed, both knowing that wasn't likely. Not in this family. "So, I've got to run up to Ocracoke today to pick up the countertops for the kitchen."

"What?" Disappointment crushed me. We hadn't had a day together in months, just the two of us, and he'd promised we could spend the day at the beach, with a dinner date out tonight. "What about the beach? You promised me—no work today."

"I know. But the deal on the counters was too good to pass up. I had to grab it. Part of the deal is pickup only, they won't deliver and shipping was going to take weeks."

"You won't be back until at least dinner." I pouted. Admittedly, childish. But that's how I felt.

He stood up and grabbed his phone and keys from the coffee table, and kissed the top of my head.

"I know baby, I'm sorry. I'll make it up to you, I promise! Oh and hey, the wood for the bookcases is being delivered to the cottage today. Can you head over there in about thirty minutes, so you can sign for the delivery?"

"Alright." I rolled my eyes. "Want me to start building, too?" That was sarcasm, and he knew it.

"I love it when you're sassy with me." He jumped off the porch and got into his truck, waving with a wink before he pulled down the driveway.

I huffed and puffed a bit as I stood up, and stepped into my sandals. Thirty minutes was more than enough time for me to head over there. I figured it was a good opportunity to take a few more measurements. I wanted to start ordering rugs for the bedrooms. The renovation was almost complete, and once the kitchen was finished we were planning to move in. The part of renovation I'd been waiting for was finally here, decorating, making the house our home. Penny and I had it all planned out, from paint colors to greenery for the mantel.

I jumped into the Jeep and drove out the driveway toward Cottage Row. I'd always loved being on our property, and I was looking forward to moving into our house, and still being here. Every day when I'd leave or come back, I would imagine what was to come. Port and Penny and the boys were long settled in the main house, and I found myself excited to watch the boys grow there. Port had the dream: the family, the home, and his work on the estate that he loved more each day. I just hoped that Hobie and I would have the same joy tomorrow and eighty years from now as we do today. The same joy that everyone else here shares so deeply, and so intertwined with one another.

I pulled into my driveway, and was caught off guard by the flower pots and window boxes that had been set perfectly across the front porch. I didn't know Penny was already planning on starting our to do list. White gypsophila lined the windows and the pots filled the porch and the stairs with brilliant shades of pink, which fit in perfectly with the azaleas that were blooming in the front yard. I was planning to start planting the front landscape over the next few weeks, and now it was done.

I got out of the jeep, staring at the floral overload in the front yard. It was perfect. I stopped at the edge of the sidewalk, in front of the mailbox. The old rusted steel box had been replaced. The stained wood post held a new white mailbox; *The Logan Family* painted in navy blue. *The Logan Family... Hobie Logan... his family?*

I glanced up to the porch, to see Hobie standing there, with a smile plastered across his face bigger than I'd ever seen before. I peeked at the handprints we had laid in the freshly paved sidewalk before I walked to him, and up the steps, reaching for his hands that were reached out for mine.

"What do you think?" He asked.

"I think..." I had to catch my breath. "I think it's perfect! What about the countertops?" I asked, confused.

"I got those last week. It's been really hard to keep you out of here the past few days, and yesterday I about died trying to keep you on the Erv so you wouldn't find them all working out front here."

"So you weren't feeling nauseous?" I asked.

"No." He laughed. "But it worked." I smacked his shoulder.

I caught Hobie's eyes as he glanced over my shoulder, and the corner of his mouth turned up as he fought off a smile. I turned to see what he was looking at.

My family, along the street in front of the house. In front of our home. Port, Penny, and the boys. Mom, dad, Uncle Eddy. Aunt Allison and a few others who were peeking in from the cafe porch.

"Hobie—"

"Ruby, I spent a really long time just trying to survive. I spent years... trying to figure out how to be alone, because I'd only ever been left. Tomorrow doesn't matter when you're all alone. So, I didn't know what it meant to look forward to forever, until I met you."

I heard Penny sniff and muffle her tears behind me, and I reached up to wipe my own.

"When I had it all figured out, how I was going to be alone for the rest of time, your brother stepped in and convinced me to try something else. He brought me here... to you. You taught me that lonely is a sorry way to be. I learned that enjoying the life and love I have is worth the risk, and now... I don't spend my time worrying about being alone, because I'm too busy loving you."

I laughed, wiping a few more tears. I couldn't even speak.

"Do you love me?" he asked.

I nodded, wiping my face again.

"Will you do something for me, then?"

"Did you just quote Landon Rollins Carter?" I asked.

Hobie reached into his pocket, pulling out a small gray velvet box.

"Did it work?" He dropped to his knee, and opened the box, lifting it to me.

"Yes!" I laughed.

"Yes, it worked? Or yes, you'll marry me?" He pulled my hand toward him, sliding the brightest, most beautiful round solitaire diamond onto my ring finger.

"Yes and yes!" I shrieked, pulling my hand up for a closer look. Hobie stood up and pulled me toward him, lifting me up for a kiss.

Clapping and cheering grew loud from behind us, as we celebrated our engagement on the front porch of our home. The man I loved, who came here only knowing how to leave, just asked me to stay forever. Saying yes was the easiest decision I'd ever made.

My dad and uncle Eddy swooped in and everyone else followed behind them.

"Atta boy." Uncle Eddy said, throwing his arm around Hobie's shoulder.

"Oh my goodness, it's stunning!" Penny said as she pulled my hand almost into her eyes.

"Hobie, is there food?" Roy interjected.

"Royal Dixon. Can you be chill for like, a second?" Penny answered.

"You bet there is." Hobie answered. "Everyone come on in. We've got brunch all set up in the kitchen."

"You do?" I asked. I couldn't believe it all.

"That's not all we have." Port added, opening the front door.

I followed Hobie inside, and held my breath as I took it all in. The house was complete. The rugs that Penny and I had chosen were already laid out underneath the furniture. Pictures were framed and hung perfectly along the walls, with a print of my own across the fireplace mantle.

I spun around, soaking up every inch of the place I could see. I stopped when I faced the door again, when I saw the frame on the wall just to the right of the door, above a row of hooks for our keys—a few of which were already hanging. It was the drawing. The one I started, way back when he first mentioned helping with renovations. Only now, it had been finished, seemingly step-by-step all along. It had every detail we'd talked about over the last year. He must have been listening and drawing it out the whole time. I stepped closer and looked at the details in the photo.

There was a ring drawn on the front porch. Cribs drawn in the bedrooms. A boat docked in the back. Next to this picture was another, an old picture of Uncle Eddy, Aunt Nori, my mom and dad. They were all laughing, at who knows what. It was a

THE ESTATE

picture I hadn't seen before. I stepped closer and reached up, drawing my finger underneath the four of them. It felt like I was almost reaching back in time, back to when Aunt Nori was still here. I wish she'd known Hobie.

"Welcome home, Ruby." Uncle Eddy stepped up behind me, resting his hands on my shoulders, and kissing the top of my head. Tears fell faster than I could dry them.

We walked through the living room and into the kitchen, which smelled like homemade chocolate chip cookies. Penny stepped around us, and pulled a fresh tray from the oven.

Uncle Eddy, dad, and the boys climbed up onto the stools at the island. Aunt Allison poured coffee into mugs. Sam and Roy dove into the cinnamon rolls in front of them, each swiping a finger of icing off the top.

Hobie stepped up close behind me, and gently rubbed the back of my neck as we watched everyone. When he leaned forward and kissed my cheek, I knew I had it all.

"Welcome home, baby." Hobie said.

I turned to face him, and took a deep breath.

"Speaking of baby..."

THE ESTATE

The Wrightsville Series

The entire series is available now on Amazon in paperback and Kindle edition.

This series may be complete, but don't go far. There are new stories coming your way. You can be the first to hear about new releases by following Annalee Thomasson on Amazon.

Made in USA - Kendallville, IN
25866_9798683894955
06.17.2022 1306